UNBREAKABLE DEUX

BY

DIANA CARTER

UNBREAKABLE DEUX

DIANA CARTER

P.O. Box 300795
Drayton Plaines, MI 48330
ldtpllc@gmail.com

OTHER BOOKS WRITTEN BY DIANA CARTER

BROKEN PROMISES SERIES

Broken Promises: Shattered Dreams
When Shattered Dreams Become Reality
Shattered Dreams The Final Chapter
In The Name of Justice: The Erica Blackstone Chronicles

DARK REVENGE SERIES

The Trey Taylor Story
When Time Runs Out: Tara's Quest for Vengeance
TJ The Forgotten Brother

The Sister Factor Series

Diamond's Fight for Justice
Dior's Darlings Daycare
Kristina's Kozy Korner
Krystal's House of Secrets
Never a Dull Moment: The Nick Jr. Story

Single Titles

The Candidate: The Race to the Top
Unbreakable: When Two Hearts Become One
The Making of a Legend: Neek's Rise to Fame

<u>Dedication</u>

It's that time again. Another exciting sequel under the author's writing belt. ***Unbreakable Deux*** the sequel to ***Unbreakable: When Two Hearts Become One*** is the story about the twin sister that gave the main character in the first book (Naomi) unbelievable grief. As I move forward in my writing career, I would like to give praise to God for giving me the creativity to continue to write about the lives of such rich characters. I dedicate this book to my readers. Over the years you all have shown me so much love and support. Look for bigger and better things in the coming years.

<u>Acknowledgements</u>

God as my Lord and Savior has been through this journey with me while I thought about the characters, plots, and genres of each book that have been written. At times everything just falls into place (***Broken Promises, Dark Revenge, and The Sister Factor***) series. Other times it's difficult to bring to life a book that is entertaining and enjoyable to read (***The Candidate***). It's moving that in the end it all comes together. ***Unbreakable Deux*** was a challenge because it was the first book I've written about an interracial couple.

I would like to take the time to acknowledge a special lady that was kind enough to give me positive feedback about ***Unbreakable Deux*** and the rewrites of my first four books ***Broken Promises*** books 1-3 and ***Dark Revenge*** book 1, Donna Brown. Donna gave me food for thought when it came to characters and storylines. It was so enlightening receiving feedback from Donna. As I continue to write, I hope my future books bring joy and entertainment to my present and future readers. Look for the sequel to ***The Making of a Legend: Neek's Rise to Fame*** and book three in the ***Unbreakable*** series to be published next year (2020).

God's blessing,

Diana Carter

Chapter One

The time had finally come. After two important events that were a disaster because the two feuding families refused to get along, London and Greg decided it was time to put all their cards on the table. Over the past few months the families attempted to come to terms and co-exist, but their attempts were big failures. Reaching their breaking point with the wedding only a month away, this meeting was arranged to let the families know they will not tolerate the disrespect both sides have shown. The couple threatened to move away and not speak to their families if there was no resolution between the families from today's meeting.

London sat in her car trying to work up the nerve to enter the building where they were meeting. She thought just a year ago this was the same building that her twin brother, Logan and sister-in-law Naomi had their wedding reception. That was such a happy time for the families. The trouble London caused Naomi in the past was nothing compared to the harassment London received from Greg's family, especially his twin sister Gracey. The rest of Greg's family (parents' Greg Sr. and Gloria, younger brother, Glenn, and uncle, Grant his dad's twin brother) wasn't happy about the relationship either.

London couldn't understand why the family was being so mean to her since this wasn't Greg's first interracial relationship. Six months before they met Greg had broken up with a Chinese woman he had been dating for two years. As matter of fact he hadn't dated a white woman since he broke up with his high school sweetheart his junior year in college. He dated a few black women but never took them around his family. He had even brought Latino women around his family. Of course, they had problems with that too but not to the extent they were having with London. Then she thought maybe it had something to do with her short marriage to Troy Tyson a few years back. Greg explained to London it was because he was never serious with the other women from the past. He said his family felt they were moving too fast in their relationship.

They had to rent space to have the meeting because of the families never ending bickering. Both sides of the families thought their homes were more suitable for the showdown. It was the same with the church homes. The families went around in circles about where London and Greg should be married. In the end they decided on the couple being married in London's family church with the reception being held in the fellowship hall at Greg's family church. The two families haven't been together since Greg's birthday dinner over two months ago. London was so lost in her thoughts she nearly jumped out of her skin when Greg knocked on her window to get her attention.

"What are you trying to do give me a heart attack?" London asked.

"Of course, not sweetheart. I wouldn't do that to you. Then I would have to go in there alone to face that group of angry people." Greg responded.

"So that is the only reason you need me alive? To save you from our feuding families." London asked jokingly.

"No. Let's go sweetheart. We can't put this off any longer." That was all Greg said as he helped London out of her car then lead her into the Lion's Den.

Once they were inside the building they took a deep breath and headed to the meeting room. As they figure would happen, the families were sitting on different sides of the room. When the families noticed that London and Greg had arrived, the moms headed towards them. They seemed to race each other to see who would get to the couple first.

"Mother, I thought we had an understanding. We are at the end of our rope dealing with you guys acting like spoiled selfish children." Greg said to his mom in a stern voice.

"Gregory, I will not be spoken to like an unruly child." Gloria responded.

"Then stop acting as such. This is the last meeting we intend to have with you guys. If you all don't come to terms to our satisfaction by the conclusion of this meeting we're done." Greg said.

For the first time since rushing up to her daughter, Lori spoke directly to London. "What the hell is he talking about London?"

"Stop being disrespectful, Ma. You will call Greg by his name. We are so fed up with keep having to address these issues. We have tried to be patient because we understand this is a big adjustment for both families, but you all need to grow up and accept our relationship or leave us alone." London said angrily.

"What I'm talking about, Ms. Lori is that London and I will no longer tolerate our families putting their noses where they don't belong. We are getting married. It's supposed to be a happy occasion but all of you are making it as difficult as possible."

"May I see you alone for a minute, London?" Lori asked ignoring Greg's tirade.

"No, you may not, Ma. We are going in there to talk about this situation as adults." London answered. She took Greg's hand then entered the room where everyone was waiting. Her mom and Gloria followed close behind.

Once London and Greg were closer to the others in the room, they went to the front, so everyone could see them. London and Greg looked around the room shaking their heads. They had talked about this situation more than once and each time the results were the same. The families seemed dead set against closing the gaps in their relationships. London was proud of Logan and Naomi because they worked hard to help London with trying to bridge the families together. During these hard times Naomi was her rock. London didn't know how Naomi could be so forgiving of her past actions, but she was grateful that Naomi had such a forgiving heart. Clearing her throat London began to speak.

"Thank you all for coming out this evening. I wish this was for a joyous occasion but the past behaviors of most of the people in this room has led to this showdown."

"We have decided this is the last chance we are going to give our families to put your differences aside. London and I are on the verge of canceling our wedding plans." Greg chimed in.

"That's the best news you have given us over the last year or so twin." Gracey said not knowing what was coming next.

"I think you have misunderstood what I mean about canceling the wedding, Gracey. We are most certainly still getting married, it's just we will do it alone and away from all of you guys." Greg corrected.

"Are you insane. There has never been an elopement in the Gordon family. You're not going to start." Gloria said with an attitude.

"Mother you are mistaken if you think anyone in this room can dictate how London and I choose to spend the rest of our lives. We would like to give you guys food for thought. If you guys don't come to terms before we leave this room tonight, London and I are already in the process of moving away with no intentions of returning." Greg threatens.

The shocked faces in the room said it all. "I know you're not cutting your family off to be with this tramp, twin?" Gracey asked.

"I suggest you leave this room right now, Gracey or I will show you better than I can tell you what happens to people who let their mouth get them into more trouble than they can handle." London replied.

"Nephew, I know you're not going to let that woman stand there and threaten your sister?" Grant said.

"What I'm going to do, Uncle Grant is to ask my rude sister to leave if she can't show London the respect she deserves." Greg responded.

"Listen everyone. I suggest all of you to calm down. Are you ready to lose London and Greg? They are putting all their cards on the table." Naomi said trying to calm the situation.

"I agree with my baby sister. There is no love lost between London and I, but she and Greg have a right to live their lives the way they see fit." Colby added.

"This coming from a woman who changes her men as often as she changes her clothes." Gloria said.

"Everybody cut this nonsense out right now. Grant, Gloria, and Gracey, you all need to realize what you are doing. I'm not losing my daughter because you guys want to act like idiots. I will ensure you that my family will meet you half way in calling a truce. We all made mistakes dealing with their relationship but in the end, nothing is worth me losing my baby girl." Logan Sr. said.

"Son, we will work this out amongst us. You don't have to leave. Your uncle, mom, and sister have a lot to learn about compassion. Logan Sr., I will get together with my family to arrange for a small dinner party for just the families. Greg and London have too much on their plates already to try to referee between us." Greg Sr. said.

"That can be arranged, Greg Sr." Logan Sr. went over to Greg Sr. to hand him his business card. "Call me once you put your family in check. I will do the same with mine."

"Thank you, Dad, and Mr. Greg. I really appreciate what you two are doing. We love you guys and just want to have peace between our families. We are not naïve. We know there will be challenges in our relationship from the outside world. It would be nice to know that we have our families full support."

"Dad, you're tripping. You can force feed that woman down our throats. We are grown and have a right to our own opinions." Gracey said then left the room.

"Anyone else have something to say about not wanting to work together to bridge the gap within our families?" Greg asked.

For the first time Greg's youngest brother, Glenn spoke up. "I want to apologize to you, London. I used to feel like Gracey until I realized how happy my brother has been over the last year. Welcome to the family.”

"Thank you, Glenn. I appreciate your support." London replied. "Let's call it a night. Thank you all for coming out." The families chatted for a few minutes longer before taking their leave. London and Greg stayed behind to talk to Naomi and Logan for a few minutes. They made plans to get together soon then left to go home.

Chapter Two

The next morning after the meeting with both families, London sat on her bed after calling off from work. She didn't have the energy to get herself together to make it to work. After talking to Naomi once she arrived home last night, London knew she had to face the fact that she might be pregnant. Naomi, who was nearly seven months pregnant with twins, recognized the symptoms. London knew if she was pregnant she couldn't be more than two months because she and Greg didn't make love but once after she persuaded him it was ok after her bridal shower in June. They both decided to wait to build their relationship before having sex. Naomi and Logan were good role models for them. She was proud of her brother and sister-in-law's decision to wait (although she thought they were crazy at the time).

London was involved in too many relationships in the past where sex played a significant role. Since she failed miserable in the past she wanted to try something different. This choice was hard for her and Greg since they both were used to having an active sex life. Also, a big help was going to Pastor Sanders for their premarital counseling. London was happy that she and Greg balanced each other lives by respecting their differences. To be fair they decided to have a total of six premarital counseling sessions (three with Pastor Sanders and three with Father Carson). Although Greg was raised in the Catholic church he was opened minded and knowledgeable of other religions.

London had a lot to think about her future before and after her marriage. She liked her job as an engineer and wanted to continue to work, but Greg wanted her to be a stay at home wife and mom when they started having children. One thing they had to iron out was that Greg wanted a large family (six to eight kids) while London would be satisfied with one or two. If she was pregnant now that would give Greg's family something else to hold against her. It was just her luck the one time she and Greg let their emotions get carried away she ended up pregnant. Not willing to put it off, London headed to the bathroom to take her dreaded pregnancy test.

Greg decided to pay his family a visit. He was disappointed with the way things turned out last night. The traveling to France frequently over the last few years for work had him considering maybe he and London should make France their home. He was going to surprise her for their honeymoon by taking her there, but he knew he had to give her a heads up since they were going to be gone for nearly a month. He decided to mix his honeymoon with business. London could never get away on his previous trips. She was so excited when he told her they were honeymooning in France that the wedding ceremony itself was kind of pushed to the back burner. Pulling up in his parents' driveway, Greg exited his car. He was saddened to see that his uncle was there. He had hoped to only talk to his parents and siblings. At times it was hard to take his dad and uncle on at the same time. They were like the routine good cop/bad cop (his dad was the good cop). Letting himself in he went in the direction of the voices until he entered the family room.

"Good morning family. I'm glad to see all of you could make it." Greg said.

"I hope this little pow wow isn't about me." Gracey said.

"Check yourself, sis. Not everything is about you." Glenn said.

"Go fly little boy." Gracey said angrily. She and Glenn have never gotten along.

"Cut it out you two. Why can't the two of you try to get along?" Gloria said as she watched Gracey roll her eyes at Glenn.

"Yes, it is partly about your behavior last night, Gracey. I've warned you to stop disrespecting London and her family." Greg responded.

"Have you tried telling her the same thing my dear twin? She is by far the worst person you have ever dated. Before you go ballistic, I'm not saying this because she's black, I'm saying this because it's true. You guys don't fit together." Gracey continued.

"That's not for you or anyone else in this family or London's family to decide. We are going forth with our plans whether you guys are on board or not."

"Greg, on behalf of the family, I would like to apologize for last night's disaster. We all should have behaved appropriately." Greg Sr. said.

"Sr. don't you go apologizing for me. I'm my own person and I will say it again, London isn't the right person for my nephew to build his life with. He needs a wife that isn't so aggressive" Grant said.

"With all due respect, Uncle Grant that isn't for you to decide. In case you didn't have a clear understanding last night, London and I are done with the interfering. We are of the mind to leave all of you alone because we are sick of defending our relationship."

'I can't believe you're treating us like this, twin." Gracey said in tears.

"Come off it, Gracey. You are the main one we need to get away from. I love all of you guys and wouldn't want to have to leave, but I'm done defending my relationship with London." Greg said.

"This is so not like you, Greg. You are letting that girl tear this family apart." Gloria shouted.

"Mother, you need to stop. We have all been unfair to Greg and London. Just because we may feel she isn't the right person for him in the end it's his decision." Glenn said defending his big brother.

"I see what's going on here. What kind of girl are you going to drop in our laps little boy?" Gracey asked.

"Stop calling me a little boy. That is old now and I will not tolerate you belittling me when I don't agree with you." Glenn said angrily to Gracey.

"Listen, I didn't come over here to argue with all of you. This should be a happy time for all of us but the fighting between you all is driving a wedge between London and I as well as both families. She will have a similar talk with her family."

"Well, she needs to. Her mother is crass and rude. I can see why London's twin and his family stays away from them." Gloria said.

"That's not any of our business, Mother. We have one more event to get through, the rehearsal dinner. This is the last time I'm going to ask that you all play nice." Greg said goodbye to his family. He hoped after he left, they would talk then come up with a plan of how to behave at the last event.

<u>Chapter Three</u>

London sat in her bathroom with tears running down her face. She didn't know whether to be happy or sad that the little stick she held in her hand had a positive reading. She was so glad she asked Naomi to stop by on her lunch break. She didn't know when or how to tell Greg. She looked back at that night with regret. She should have taken Logan's offer of help to get the tons of gifts she received from her bridal shower home. She was happy and surprised when Greg showed up to offer to help take her gifts home. She was still tipsy from the three or four drinks she had and didn't care about their agreement to wait before they had a sexual relationship. She remembered how Greg kept trying to stop her, but she persisted. He told her he didn't have protection, but she said that was okay because it wasn't her fertile time of the month.

Now she was going to have to worry about if he would feel that she was trying to trap him. She wished Naomi would hurry up and get there. The things going on in her mind were driving her crazy. If Greg's sister and mom found out before the wedding they will swear up and down that she trapped Greg. That is why she was leaning on the side of not telling Greg about the baby until after the wedding. She also was wondering if her being pregnant would have to change any of the plans Greg made for their honeymoon. She was so excited with what he'd told her so far about their honeymoon. The glint in his eyes said that he had something exciting in store for them.

The buzzing sound brought London out of her daydreaming. She went to the keypad in her hallway to let Naomi in. Seeing her sister-in-law wobbling into her apartment made London fearful. She didn't know if she was ready to be a mom. The big smile on Naomi's face brought calm to London. Once they were seated in the kitchen Naomi started the conversation.

"I can tell by the look on your face you took the test."

"Yes, I did. You were right, I'm pregnant." London confirmed.

"How do you feel about it, London?" Naomi asked.

"Scared to death. I don't know if I'm ready to be a mom. We only have one more session of premarital counseling with Pastor Sanders. I was sitting here thinking if I should wait until after the wedding to tell Greg."

Naomi was shaking her head. "I don't think that is a good idea. You're not thinking straight. What you may want to do first is to go to your doctor to confirm your test results." Naomi advised.

London smiled for the first time since waking up. "Oh, that's a great idea. Maybe the test is a false positive."

"So, you're not happy to be starting a family?" Naomi asked.

"Not with all our other issues. I know Gracey is God's way of paying me back for all the bad things I did to you. That chick just won't let up."

"God isn't in the business of punishing people. Gracey has deep seeded issues that her family needs to address."

Suddenly London started crying. "Naomi, I'm so sorry for the way I treated you. I was so mean and miserable. I was jealous of the relationship you had with Logan."

"Let's leave the past where it belongs. We all have our bad moments. I know you're scared, London but don't let that get in the way of all the good in your life."

"Oh God. Ma is going to be on her high horse. I'm not telling anyone if it's true. You can tell Logan, but he has to promise not to tell anyone else."

"London, we have to take this one step at a time. Make an appointment with your doctor. I will go with you. The sooner the better. Again, I advise you to tell Greg. You can go into marriage with a big secret like this."

"I don't know if I can do that, Naomi. The one and only time we had sex I pressured him. He didn't have a condom, but I told him it wasn't a fertile time of the month. Even to my ears that sounds like entrapment."

"What you said may have been a deciding factor, but he still had a choice to wait." Naomi said.

"I know you're right. Thanks for coming over. I know you need to get back to the office. You're going to have to get off your feet soon because those babies are going to come early if you keep working so hard."

"Time to go. You're sounding like your brother now."

London walked Naomi to the door then went back into her bedroom to ponder what she was going to do if she was pregnant.

While London and Naomi were having their talk, Logan was sitting at a table with Greg. Logan was kind of surprised to get a call from Greg out of the blue. He never had a one-on-one with Greg. After ordering their lunch Greg started the conversation. "I know you may be wondering why I wanted to meet with you."

"Yes, you made this sound so mysterious." Logan replied.

"I felt it was time we got to know each other better. I know London loves all of her family, but she has a close relationship with you that means the world to her."

"Yes, we are close."

"Logan, I may not be the person you would choose to be with your sister, but I love her with all my heart. I want to spend the rest of my life making her happy."

"Honestly, you're not what I expected. It's not just the race difference but also your personality is a lot different from the men London is used to dating.

"Thank you for being honest, Logan. It seems like our families are never going to agree to get along. That is the reason I wanted to reach out to you."

"I'm listening."

"London and I are serious about moving away if we can't have peace here. I think she would love France. Since I have to travel there frequently maybe we have to make our home there."

Logan didn't like the idea of his sister moving to another country. "Have you spoken to London about this?"

"Not about France, but we have talked about moving away. She wants to stay here and so do I."

"Well that is what you should do. You don't have to move to find peace. You just need to set ground rules for the families to follow. I know that will be difficult because Naomi and I had to go through the same thing when we got back together."

"It's amazing the relationship London has with Naomi. I couldn't believe it when London told me all the awful things, she did in the past to keep the two of you apart. Naomi is a very special person to be so forgiving."

"She is beyond special. Life hasn't been easy for her, but she always finds a way to get through the many crisis in her life."

"Let's eat before our food gets cold. I hope you don't mind if I continue to reach out to you. I want to make peace with your family." Greg said as they decided to table their conversation to finish their lunch, so they could get back to work.

<u>Chapter Four</u>

London sat at her doctor's office waiting on her blood and urine work to come back. She was so glad that Naomi took the day off from work. They were going back to Naomi's house to work on the nursery after they were done at the clinic. London was so nervous about the test results she canceled her dinner plans with Greg the night before. She tried to sound as cheerful as possible when she talked to him. Greg picked up something was bothering her, but she played it off to wedding nerves. Hearing her name called she followed the nurse into the doctor's office and asked Naomi to go in with her. Once they were seated the doctor began.

"London after reviewing your blood and urine samples, it's official you're pregnant." Seeing the look of defeat on London's face the doctor continued. "So, I take it this wasn't a planned pregnancy?"

"No, it wasn't. I'm about to get married in a few weeks. You don't have to wonder about the due date. I was only with my fiancé once."

"I remember now. You said that the two of you decided to wait until after you were married to have a sexual relationship."

"We were doing good with that too until I had too much to drink at my bridal shower and convinced Greg that we would be okay because it wasn't my fertile time."

"Why didn't you use protection?"

"Because he didn't have any and I didn't want to wait. Now I don't know what to do or if I should tell him because he may think I tricked him." London said with tears falling down her face.

"London, I told you everything is going to be ok. Greg is a reasonable man. He played a part in this so he can't completely blame you." Naomi said trying to calm London down.

"Since the deed is already done you need to figure out in a hurry what your plans are. According to the date you gave me in a few more weeks you will be out of your first trimester." The doctor said.

"I'm going to have my baby doctor. I just don't know if I will have a husband."

"I think it's time for us to head out of here, London. What's next for London to do doctor?" Naomi asked.

"Set up your next appointment before you go on your honeymoon and I will send your prescription in for prenatal vitamins and iron pills."

"Thank you, doctor. I will see you in a few weeks." London said.

"Try to stay calm and talk it over with your fiancé." The doctor said.

London and Naomi left the clinic once she made her appointment. London thought she was going to need her brother and sister-in-law more than ever.

London decided to stay over at Naomi and Logan's house until Logan returned home. Naomi asked him to come straight home from work. She was glad their daughter, Sierra was having a stayover at her friend's house. Sierra was a good girl but at times she asked too many questions. London was in no shape to answer her niece's inquisitive questions. London had just gotten up from taking a nap a few minutes before Logan arrived home. Taking one look at his sister he knew all was not right in her world. He hoped it didn't have anything to do with Greg. He still was uncomfortable about sharing his lunch date with Greg to his sister. Naomi told him it was his call and she would support his decision.

"Wow, sis. I'm surprised you tore yourself away from your boo." Logan said jokingly.

"Baby, London has something she needs to discuss with you. I will get us some snacks since it will be an hour or so before dinner is ready." Naomi said as she left the twins to talk.

"Ok, Lon what's wrong?" Logan asked.

"I messed up and now I don't know if Greg is going to dump me." London's eyes were glassy from her unshed tears.

"Sis stop talking silly. I had lunch with Greg the other day. That man is hopelessly in love with you." Logan said.

"I have something to tell you, but you can't tell anyone. I only want you and Naomi to know."

"I don't like the sound of this. If this has anything to do with your relationship with Greg, then he has a right to know."

"I need you to promise me you won't tell Greg or anyone else, Lo." The twins reverted to their childhood names they used to call each other.

"What's going on, Lon. I'm worried about you." Logan asked.

"You remember the night of my bridal shower when you picked Naomi up and asked if I needed a ride home. I told you no because Greg showed up unexpectedly, so I just had him to take me home."

"Yes, that was a few months back." Logan said.

"Well, Greg took me home, but I had one too many drinks. As you know we were doing the no sex thing until we tied the knot."

"Ok. Go on."

"I don't know what came over me, but I didn't want to wait any longer. Greg tried to talk me down because we didn't have any protection. I persuaded him that we would be fine because it wasn't my fertile time of the month."

"Oh no, Lon. Please tell me that you're not pregnant."

"I took a test a few days ago and went to the doctor this morning and she confirmed that I am." This time London was sobbing.

"What did Greg say. I know he's not talking crazy." Logan said going into his protective mode.

"He hasn't said anything because I haven't told him, and I don't know if I can. He's going to think I trapped him."

"Why the hell haven't you told him, Lon?"

"I just told you why. I was thinking about waiting until after the wedding."

"That's not a smart move, Lon."

"What if I tell him before the wedding then he walks out on me?"

"If he does that stupid shit, I will tell him to stay the hell out of your life after I kick his ass." Logan said.

"You can't blame all this on him, Lo."

"The hell I can't. You guys should have waited but since you didn't you have to deal with the consequences. He didn't have to do it, so he has to take some of the responsibility."

Naomi walked into the room with a tray. Logan hurried to help her. "Logan you need to calm down. I heard you shouting all the way in the kitchen."

"Baby, I guess you know all about this?" Logan said to his wife.

"Yes, I do. I told London she had to tell Greg right away."

"I agree, but why didn't you tell me what was going on?"

"I asked her to wait until we had confirmation so don't get your shorts in a bunch." London said.

"Let's table this for now. We can eat dinner. London, I think you should stay the night with us, if not Logan can drive you home. You need support right now. You also need to think about talking to Greg and your parents about this situation." Naomi said.

"Oh no. I'm not going to let Ma know how stupid I was. I will think about telling Greg but that's it."

"That's your decision, Lon. Let's just have a quiet dinner together." Logan said.

<u>Chapter Five</u>

It's been a few days since London had dinner with Naomi and Logan. She knew it was time to come clean with Greg about her pregnancy. He demanded to see her right away since she canceled yet again another dinner with him last night. London went to work yesterday, but she didn't feel like being there. She forced herself to go in since she would be taking four weeks off for her honeymoon (at least she hoped she was still getting married after coming clean to Greg). Now as she set the table for their dinner, London prayed their talk will go well. She was getting a late start because she decided to think back to the time when she and Greg first met.

London was mad from another run in with Naomi. She wished her brother would wise up and drop that chick. Naomi was so controlling and demanding, London didn't know how Logan could put up with it. London knew in her heart she was jealous of the strong bond between Logan and Naomi. She was so into her thoughts she didn't realize until it was too late that she was headed into the wrong restroom in the crowded Panera Bread. Colliding into the most handsome man she'd seen in a long time startled London.

"I'm sorry. I wasn't looking where I was going." London apologized to the stranger.

"No worries. Are you okay? You look upset." The stranger responded.

"I'm fine. I just want to knock some sense into my twin brother who is about to marry an ice princess." London responded.

"Oh, my we have something in common. I have a twin sister that drives me looney sometimes."

"He is such a great man. I don't want him to settle when he can do so much better." London continued.

"Now that is something you and my twin sister have in common. No matter whom I'm with she feels that there is someone better out there to scoop me up."

"Wait a minute. I'm not interfering in my brother's life. I just want what is best for him and Ms. Naomi cold as ice Nichols isn't cutting it."

"Are you in a hurry. I would love to chat with you a bit longer. By the way my name is Greg Gordon Jr."

"I'm London Lewis. Good to meet you, Greg. My table is in the back corner. It has bridal magazines on it. I'll meet you there in a few minutes."

London smiled. She and Greg talked for over an hour and exchanged numbers. He had recently broken up from a serious two year relationship. London was surprised to find out his previous relationship was with a Chinese woman. Greg came off as a stuffy stuck up Caucasian man. As they got to know each other their relationship grew into something very special. From the beginning Greg warned London his family will not be supportive of their relationship, especially his twin sister Gracey. That didn't matter because for the first time in her life, she found someone she felt really cared about her. Her dad and brother had always been the two most important men in her life until she met Greg.

From her first-time meeting Gracey, London knew what she did to Naomi in the past was coming back to bite her in the behind. Gracey was more than protective of Greg, she was downright obsessive. She would play nice when Greg was around but once they were alone the witch in Gracey would come out. At one point London thought about telling Greg what Gracey was doing but thought better because she was just getting what she put out. The rest of Greg's family wasn't much better. His Uncle Grant (dad's twin brother) was like the male version of Gracey.

London took time to think about her family's reaction. Unreal enough Naomi was the first person she told about Greg. It was during the time she first realized she had to make amends with Naomi or lose her brother. Now they were good friends. So much so if Naomi wasn't so far along in her pregnancy she would have been London's matron of honor. Instead London's best friend Makayla was her maid of honor. Hearing the door bell brought London back to earth. She was nervous at the thought that tonight may be her last night as an engaged woman and she would end up a statistic: a single parent. Waiting for Greg at the door was the scariest thing she had to face in a long time. Opening the door to the relieved look on Greg's face calmed London's nerves.

"My God, sweetheart it is so good to see you. I've been going crazy thinking that you were working up the nerve to call our wedding off." Greg said.

"Why would you think something crazy like that, Greg?" London asked.

"It feels like I haven't seen you in forever. What's going on in your life to make you keep cancelling our plans?"

"Let's eat before we get into all of that. I made your favorites." Greg's favorites consisted of corn beef, cabbage, potato salad, and sourdough bread.

"Sure, thing sweetheart. I didn't think I was hungry until I walked in here."

London and Greg headed to the dining room where the table had already been set. Once they were done eating to kill time London asked Greg to wait for her in the living room while she cleaned up. Joining Greg twenty minutes later with coffee, tea, and croissants, London sat her tray on the table then sat down next to Greg on the loveseat.

"London, I get the feeling that you are nervous about something. Sweetheart you can talk to me about anything. I love you so much, sweetheart." Greg said.

"I love you too, baby."

"I have your back, London. Whatever is on your mind, we will handle it together."

"Okay." Pausing for a few seconds, London started up again. "Greg, we have been through so much with both of our families. I just want everything to be perfect for us."

"We're on the right track, London so don't worry about what's ahead."

"Greg, I made an error in judgement. I hope this won't affect our relationship."

"You're scaring me sweetheart. Just tell me what's gotten you so upset."

"I have been feeling under the weather over the last few weeks. I was talking to Naomi and she suggested I go see my doctor."

"Please don't tell me you're ill, sweetheart."

"No, Greg, but I'm pregnant."

Greg looked at London like she had grown another head. "I'm sure I didn't hear you correctly. You said you're pregnant?"

"Yes, I did."

"What the hell, London. How could you do this to me?"

"I didn't do this by myself, Greg."

"Don't be coy with me, London. Who else have you been seeing?"

"I know you didn't go there, Greg."

"Where else do you expect me to go when you give me news like that. We haven't been together sexual so you're sitting here telling me you're pregnant is a big deal."

"What the hell do you mean we haven't been together. Are you forgetting what happened after my bridal shower?"

Greg thought for a moment as recognition flashed across his face. "Wait a minute, that was just one time and you told me it wasn't your fertile time of the month."

"By my calculations it shouldn't have been."

"So, you're saying that is when this happened?"

"Of course, that is what I'm saying. That is the one and only time we were together."

"London this isn't making any sense. You're trying to tell me this is my child."

The hurt look that crossed London's face went past Greg. As silent tears rolled down her face, London took a deep breath and said, "It's time for you to leave, Greg."

"We're not done with this discussion, London."

"Yes, we are. Please leave." London stood then walked to her bedroom and slammed the door.

Chapter Six

London woke up the next morning with her eyes feeling so heavy she could hardly open them. She cried so much last night she didn't think she could shed another tear. Last night after she left the room, she heard Greg leave her apartment. About an hour later the phone wouldn't stop ringing. When she checked it a couple of times it was Greg. She had nothing to say to him, so she didn't answer. Then she started getting calls from her family. She was tempted to answer Naomi and Logan's calls, but she couldn't bring herself to fill them in on what happened between her and Greg. Eventually the calls stopped but started back this morning waking her up. She just wished everyone would leave her alone.

Lying in her bed with silent tears rolling down her face, London was shaken from her dreary state when she heard movements in her apartment. She knew it had to be Naomi or Logan or both because they were the only ones that had access and a key to her apartment. The slight knock on her door answered the question to her thoughts when Naomi asked if she could come in. Not wanting to talk but knowing she had to, London told Naomi to come in.

"London are you okay? Greg said we needed to come by to check on you since you weren't answering your phone."

"I don't feel like talking right now, Naomi. I will give you a call later."

"That's not going to work. Logan is here, and he isn't going to leave until he knows that you are okay."

"Please, Na. I promise to call you guys later. I just need some time alone." London sometimes shortened Naomi's name.

"What happened last night with Greg, London?"

"I see you're not going to listen to me. Give me a few minutes. I will come out to talk to you guys. You should be at church not here." After Naomi left the room, London went to the bathroom to freshen up. Once she was done, she joined Naomi and Logan in the living room.

"Good morning, Lo. You guys should be at church. Where's Sierra?" London asked.

"Mom and Dad took her to church. What happened, Lon?" Logan asked.

When London started sobbing Naomi went to sit next to her while Logan started pacing the living room floor.

"No, you stay away from me, Naomi. I shouldn't have listened to you. Now I'm going to have to be a single mom." London said angrily.

"Wait a damn minute, Lon. You're not going to blame this on Naomi. You did the right thing. What did that fool say to you?"

"He doesn't believe the baby is his." London said once she stopped sobbing.

"I'm sorry to hear that, London and that your talk with Greg didn't go well. When you asked for my advice, I gave you the best answer I could. I still believed you did the right thing, but I'm sorry you are hurting right now." Naomi said.

I'm sorry, Naomi. I didn't mean to lash out at you. I know Greg will come around. It just hurts that he would jump to that conclusion."

"Baby do you want to go ahead to church? I have something I have to take care of. Or better yet why don't you stay here with Lon and I will tell Ma and Dad to take Sierra home with them." Logan said.

"Stop it with the cave man stuff, Lo. You're going to stay out of this. I can handle this without your help." London said.

"You know I'm not going to let that punk get away with this." Logan responded.

"I said I got this, Lo. What I need is for both of you to go on to church. Greg and I will work this out."

"Honey, London is right. She needs to take care of this situation. Look at how many obstacles we had to overcome to be together."

"So, is the wedding off? If he's acting this way now how can you depend on him being there for you when you really need him?" Logan asked.

"No, the wedding isn't off. I will give him a few days to calm down then we will work through this."

"Ma and Dad are going to have a fit."

"No, they're not, Lo because you're not going to tell them anything."

"When are you planning on telling them about the baby, Lon?"

"When I get back from my honeymoon." London responded.

"Are you crazy. They should be told right away."

"Why? I remember you keeping things from the family when you and Na got back together."

"Have it your way, Lon. Let us know if you need anything."

"I will come back after church. Logan and Sierra can head home to get dinner started." Naomi said letting Logan know she expected him to leave the situation alone. Heading for the door, Naomi and Logan gave London a brief hug and headed to church.

Greg woke up Sunday morning feeling like he had a hangover even thought he hadn't had anything to drink. He still couldn't get over the news London shared with him. He knew he handled the situation all wrong. He wished he could redo his reaction. The hurt look on London's face broke his heart. He knew she hadn't been with anyone else, but he was upset that he couldn't control himself on that faithful night. The thought never crossed his mind that he would get London pregnant by having sex with her only one time. He had gone without so long and wanted to be with London so badly that at that point in time he didn't care about not having protection. They had already had a complete medical exam to make sure they both were clean.

This wasn't as bad as it seemed last night. Getting started right away on their family was a good thing. With London only wanting to have a few children he had to be grateful that she was willing to keep their child. Hearing the phone ring, he ignored it because he didn't want to talk to anyone but London. He knew Gracey was going to have a fit when she found out that London was pregnant. She will be on another "Stop the Wedding" campaign again. Thinking about the wedding, Greg hoped London wouldn't change her mind about the wedding after his poor reaction last night. Greg was interrupted from his thoughts when someone began banging on his door. Going to answer it and seeing Gracey wasn't something he wanted to deal with right now.

"Have you lost your mind banging on my door like you're the police?" Greg said to his twin sister.

"Answer your damn phone if you don't want people to pop up on your sorry behind." Gracey responded.

"Most people with common sense would know to leave me the hell alone if I don't answer their calls."

"What did that heifer do this time?" Gracey asked.

"Don't start, Gracey."

"I know she did something because you missed breakfast with the family this morning."

Shit, Greg thought to himself. He forgot all about the last minute breakfast their mom insisted on having. "My missing the breakfast had nothing to do with London. I worked late into the night and overslept."

"Whatever. You better come up with a better story for Mommy because she's not going to buy that load of bull."

"I don't need a better story. I'm a grown man with responsibilities that won't allow me to make last minute plans."

"What is it going to take twin for you to come to your senses before it's too late?"

"Goodbye, Gracey. I have to get ready to take care of a few important errands today."

"I'm leaving but don't think that I'm not going to find out what's going on. You still have time to get out of the mess you've gotten yourself into."

"Thanks for stopping by, Gracey." Greg walked his sister to the door then headed upstairs to get ready, so he could go straighten out the mess he created with London.

Chapter Seven

London was at work the following Tuesday after her fight with Greg. He dropped by on Sunday and Monday, but London refused to see him. London was thankful that Naomi was with her on Sunday to chase him away. She wasn't as lucky yesterday when he stopped by, but she told the front gate not to let him in. She knew she had to face him sooner rather than later but later was fine with her. She missed him, but she couldn't let him get away with treating her like she was a tramp. This time around Naomi and Logan decided to keep their advice to themselves. Outside of telling London she should tell their parents about the baby, Logan said he was staying out of her personal business.

Since she had some quiet time, London decided to think about her and Greg's first premarital session with Pastor Sanders. The pastor didn't want either of them to take lightly the potential problems they may have as an interracial couple. She and Greg choose from a list of topics to divide between Pastor Sanders and Father Carson (from Greg's church). Pastor Sanders would cover general premarital questions, challenges and do's and don'ts of interracial couples. Father Carson would cover the meaning, struggles, and difficulties of interracial couples. London remembered the struggles Naomi and Logan went through when they were taking their premarital sessions with Pastor Sanders. Adding another clergy person to the mix was frightening, but fair.

They started off the first session for three hours to cover any questions they may have and the typical premarital counseling questions. Pastor Sanders let them know they would cover relationship goals, personal habits, spiritual beliefs, finances, children, family, sex and intimacy, and most important for their circumstances conflict and communication. After the prayers were said London became nervous because she and Greg were going to have to face a lot of tough realities.

"Before we get started, I would like to say, I'm proud of both of you for making the decision not only to do premarital counseling but to come to terms with knowing that both sides of your religious backgrounds needed to be explored." Pastor Sanders said.

"Pastor, I think we are ahead of the game because we have spent countless hours going over the differences in our background and upbringing." London said.

"That is a good place to start with your relationship goals. It's important that both of you answer these questions openly and honestly. Greg why do you want to marry London?"

"Pastor Sanders, I knew from the first moment I met London there was something special about her. Our first conversation was enjoyable, and I didn't want it to end. I love London more than any woman I've been with and I want to spend the rest of my life making her the happiest person alive."

"London why do you want to marry Greg?"

"I felt a connection with Greg when we met, but I wasn't as secure as he was and that we were right for each other. I've never dated a man outside of my race, so I was leery. Once we started seeing each other frequently, I came to realize how much I love him and want to spend the rest of my life with him."

Pastor Sanders jotted down notes before he moved on to the next question. What do you want out of your life with Greg, London?"

"I want to make him happy and secure. I will work hard everyday to make sure he knows I have his back against anyone. I want to grow old with him and to share my joys and pain in the good times as well as the bad. This would make my life perfect."

"Greg your turn. From here on out after the other person answers the question it will be the next person's turn." Pastor Sanders said.

"Wow it's hard to come back after that, but I will leave no doubt in London's mind that she will come first in my life. We have and probably will always have people that won't support our relationship, but I will stay true to her no matter what."

Pastor for the sake of time, how about Greg and I tell you what we have already went over and take it from there. I see the next item on the list is personal habits. Since we're not going to live together before marriage, we have decided to share the household chores, shopping, and other errands." London said.

"As for spiritual beliefs, London and I have totally different backgrounds. Being raised as a Catholic was enlightening, but we decided to share in each other's religion so when the time comes when we have children, we can raise them with both sides of our spiritual backgrounds." Greg added.

"Let's move on to finances. Have you discussed this topic yet?"

"Yes, we have. I'm happy to say that we agree on this subject. Although we both have our own money, we will share with each other our financial endowments to enable us to preserve our assets for our later years and our children." Greg explained.

"Pastor the next topic is something we have to still iron out. We both want children, but we are at odds as to how many. I was thinking maybe two or three while Greg was thinking on a larger scale six or more." London added.

"This could become a major problem. How do you guys plan to handle the children issue?" Pastor Sanders asked.

"That is still a work in progress, Pastor Sanders. I'm willing to come down and London has agreed to think about going up a bit." Greg answered.

"That sounds reasonable. The next topic I know will be sticky, family. I don't know about your family Greg, but London comes from a family that likes to be all inclusive. Have there been issues with your families?"

"Have there ever! You know that saying, Pastor what goes around comes around. Well now is the time I must pay for all the problems I caused between Naomi and Logan. Greg's twin sister Gracey is ten times worse than I was back in the day."

Pastor Sanders laughed. "So how are you guys dealing with this issue?

"Gracey is hard to contain. She knows that there has never been a woman in my life that is as important as London. She tries her best to get me to end things before I get hurt. It doesn't help that my mom and uncle are on the same page."

"On my end Logan is supportive and so is dad, but Mom is beside herself. She drums into my head that if I have children with Greg they will suffer a cruel and depressing life."

"Have you guys thought about the challenges of raising mixed children?"

"Not in detail, but we know as long as we give our children love and support, they will be strong enough to endure the cruelties they may face from other children and adults." Greg said.

"I agree Pastor. We have a great support system between my dad, Naomi, Logan, and Greg's dad. That will be enough until the others decide to come around."

"What about your sex and intimacy life. Young couples now days seem to struggle a lot with this issue."

"Pastor, you know my background and Greg's sex life was just as active as mine. Seeing how Naomi and Logan handle this issue with their support we decided to not have sex until after we are married. It has been difficult but so far we're doing good."

"London's right. This is the best decision we could have made with all the other issues we have to face. We've had our health screenings and plan to have another one before we are married."

"Seems like you two are well ahead of the game. Are there any questions about what we discussed thus far before we move on to the final subject for today?"

"No, Pastor Sanders." London and Greg laughed because they both said this at the same time.

"Conflict and communication. I will be honest with the two of you. These issues are going to come up more often because of your different backgrounds. Devising a plan to combat a problem that could tear you apart is of the upmost importance. Greg what do you see as the biggest obstacle the two of you will have to overcome?"

"Our families." Greg answered.

"The perception of others." London answered.

"Can you explain your answer, London since we have already talked about your families?" Pastor Sanders asked.

"Like I said before I'm not used to the reactions of others, when they see Greg and I together. Sometimes I don't want to go out because the reactions of others make me uncomfortable."

"I've told London plenty of times, Pastor Sanders that she shouldn't let that bother her. People would find things to dislike about us even if we were of the same race."

"So, you're saying that London shouldn't care about what others think when they see the two of you together?" Pastor Sanders asked.

"No, I'm not saying that, Pastor Sanders. What I'm saying is that one day it won't bother her as much."

"Food for thought for our next session. London work on feeling comfortable as a couple and you Greg work on being more understanding of how London is feeling. Both of you have the right to feel the way you do but until you are secure with the situation the added tension may create a gap in communication."

"Will do Pastor." London said.

Coming back to the present London could see that she and Greg were not as settled with each other as she thought. The first bump in the road and they blow up at each other instead of sticking it out together to come up with a solution that works. She decided it was time to see if she and Greg had what it takes to be a family. She had no intention of raising her baby alone. She and Greg loved each other. They would find a way to get over this hump. She had to work this out before the families found out about her pregnancy. Gracey and Greg's Uncle Grant was going to have a field day. This would be the first real test to see if they have what it takes to be together. They overcame the friction both of their families threw at them. So instead of hiding she was ready to come out fighting not only for her and Greg but for the precious life they created.

Chapter Eight

When London talked to Greg on her lunch break, he sounded happy to hear from her. They only talked long enough for her to ask Greg to come over to her place at six o'clock, so they could talk. She left work at three o'clock, so she could take a short nap before Greg arrived. She was still feeling sluggish, but she didn't know if that had to do with the baby or what she was going through with Greg. Her short talk with Naomi helped a lot. Naomi was able to help her to filter through some of the literature she received from her doctor's office regarding her pregnancy. She hoped she wasn't having twins like Naomi. Even with her large support system, dealing with two babies at once made fear run through her veins.

Up and refreshed from her nap, London had about an hour before Greg was due to arrive. She was so tempted to ask Naomi to meet with her and Greg, but she didn't want to keep putting her brother and sister-in-law in her personal business with Greg. She had to learn to stand on her own when it came to her relationship with Greg. She knew there would be more problems as they continued their relationship. Thinking about that London had to smile when she thought back to their first premarital session with Father Carson. It was so different and less friendly than what they had with Pastor Sanders. They met in a small gloomy room next to the Father's office.

Opening with a prayer Father Carson started right into the session. "Are there any questions before we get started?" Once London and Greg answered no, Father Carson continued. "We're here today to talk about what it means to be in an interracial relationship. I know by now you have experienced reactions from people when you're out together.

"Yes, we have, Father. Some, people just stare while other shake their heads in disgust." Greg said.

"Although it's more common now days to see an interracial couple it's still hard for people to adapt, especially a white and black couple. People are more accepting when other races were involved.

"London how do you feel when you receive negative reactions from others when you're out with Greg?" Father Carson asked.

"Uncomfortable. It's better now but when we first started dating, I didn't want to go out in public because people treated us like we were axe murderers." London responded.

"How are your families adjusting to the two of you being together?" Father Carson continued.

"Not very well, Father. My mom, uncle, and sister are beside themselves. My dad is more tolerant but sometimes my mom wears him down." Greg said.

"My family is pretty much the same. They know the problems my relationship with Greg is going to bring and most of them feel like it's not worth it." London added.

"What about among yourselves? Have you guys discussed in which areas would you like the other to improve?"

"This is one of the lengthy conversations we've had, Father. I know it sometimes bothers Greg that I'm still a bit uncomfortable with people's reaction to our being together. It can get a bit overwhelming when you are getting negative reactions from your families and others." London explained.

"It's true, but I've had more experience with interracial dating. I haven't dated a woman within in my race since my high school sweetheart."

"Why is that, Greg?" Father Carson asked.

"I've dated by the way the other person makes me feel. I don't see skin color. I know this drives my family crazy, but I'm not closed mined like most of my family, especially Gracey."

"What do you guys find yourselves disagreeing about the most?"

"Family." London and Greg laughed because they answered this question at the same time.

The buzzing from the intercom brought London back to the present. She didn't realize she had been wrapped up in her thoughts for so long. Slowly walking to the door and buzzing Greg in made London's heart race. She was mad about this because up until a few days ago the thought of seeing Greg filled her heart with joy. Opening the door, Greg had a big smile on his face with flowers and chocolates in his hands.

"Hi, Greg." That was all London was able to get out even though she was happy he brought her favorite red roses.

"Sweetheart it's so good to see you. I missed you so much." Greg responded.

Taking the roses and candy, London said. "You can have a seat while I take care of these.

London took her time joining Greg in the living room. She hoped this meeting went better than their last.

"I'm so sorry sweetheart. I was totally in the wrong. I've missed you so much." Greg said.

London thought for a few minutes before she spoke. "I missed you too, Greg. I thought we were in a better place. With only one premarital session left I think we need to add more because we should have been able to talk this through without the short separation."

"I know. That was just last thing I expected to hear from you since we've only been together once."

"The guilt of that one time still eats away at me. I pressured you that night. It wasn't supposed to be my fertile time like I told you, but God had different plans for us."

"You know I want to have tons of children with you so that wasn't the problem. Unconsciously, I was thinking about my family's reaction."

"Well, that's a problem, Greg. We can't worry about what our families think about what goes on in our relationship. I'm very close to my brother and his wife, but I wouldn't let what they feel come between us. As a matter of fact, I had to threaten my brother to keep him from kicking your ass."

"I could imagine how he felt. Gracey gets on my last nerve but if someone harmed her I would be seeing red."

"Speaking of Gracey, what's going on with her these days? I haven't heard from her and that's a little frightening."

"She not letting on, but I think she has a new man in her life."

"Thank God. Maybe she will leave us alone." London didn't get a chance to say anything else because there was a knock at her door. Knowing that it had to be Naomi or Logan made her anxious. She prayed it was Naomi. Seeing her brother on the other side of the door alone made London's stomach knot up.

"What are you doing here, Lo?" London asked.

"My wife wouldn't give me any peace until I came by to check on you. She would have come herself but…" Logan stopped what he was saying when he saw Greg sitting in the living room.

"Don't start, Lo." London said.

"What the hell is he doing here, Lon?"

"We're trying to talk things through."

"Why, so he can insult you again?"

"Logan, I'm sorry. I've already apologized to London."

"Apology not accepted. Now leave."

"Lo, cut it out. This is between Greg and I."

"When he disrespected you, it became my problem. How do you think Ma and Dad are going to feel about the way he has treated you?"

Tears formed in London's eyes. "Lo, you promised you weren't going to tell them."

"I'm not, but you are. He can't get away with this kind of behavior."

"Logan, I overreacted. I love your sister more than anything. I look forward to bringing our child into this world."

"Bullshit, your first reaction was to lash out at my sister." Logan shouted.

"Lo, I got this. You need to go home and check on Naomi." London said.

"Naomi is good. Ms. Corrine and Sierra are taking good care of her until I get back home."

"I'm sure she would prefer your company over her mom's smothering."

"Fine. Greg and I will leave so you can rest."

"Greg and I still have some things to work through." London slightly grabbed Logan's arm and ushered him to the door. "I will call you guys if I need anything." Giving Logan a brief hug London closed the door behind him and went back into the living room to finish her conversation with Greg.

Chapter Nine

The rest of the week went by fast for London. It was now Friday evening. London was taking her time getting ready for the girls' night out that her best friend and maid of honor Makayla Matthews (Kayla) was planning. London was glad to spend time with Kayla to take her mind off things. Kayla had been complaining about their friendship ever since London became close to Naomi. She told London she knew she wouldn't have asked her to be maid of honor if Naomi wasn't pregnant. London knew her friend was right because Kayla represented the old dysfunctional London. Kayla was front and centered and egging London on with every bad thing she did to Naomi in the past. They almost had a falling out because London didn't want Kayla's younger sister, Maci to be part of the wedding party.

London studied herself in the mirror. She was so glad there were no signs in her weight that she was pregnant. She was so happy she didn't have morning sickness like Naomi had during her first trimester. Maybe that was a good sign she wasn't going to have twins. Deciding it was time to put those thoughts out of her mind for a while, London grabbed her sweater and purse about to head for the door when her land line phone began to ring. Heading back to her bedroom to answer it, she made it to the phone on its fourth ring.

"Hello."

"Sorry to bother you, Ms. Lewis, but you have a visitor that won't take no for an answer." Benny the doorman said.

"Who is it, Benny?"

"She said her name is Gracey Gordon and was perturbed that she wasn't on your visitor's list."

"Thanks, Benny. Send her up please." *Shit she was already running late. What the hell did this heifer want?*

Opening the door before Gracey could knock, London knew by the look on Gracey's face she was coming to start trouble. "Gracey, I was headed out. Why didn't you call before coming over?"

"I was close by so I took the chance you would be home."

"I only have a few minutes. What's on your mind?"

"I decided to take you up on your offer to be one of your bridesmaids." Gracey said.

"Gracey it's only a few weeks before the wedding. The party has already bought their dresses and accessories. If you join now, we will have to find another groomsman."

"What are you saying, I can't be in your wedding?"

"I see you're here to start trouble. We have to talk later."

"Fine. Don't say I didn't try." Gracey went to door and turned back to look at London. "I was hoping things wouldn't get this far. I guess my foolish brother is going to have to find out the hard way the error of his ways."

London shook her head after Gracey slammed her door. There was no way Gracey wanted to be part of the wedding. Greg must have threatened to cut her off or she had something else up her sleeve. Either way London didn't have time to think about what was going on with her soon to be sister-in-law. Texting Kayla that she was running late, London headed out the door to meet the girls.

Naomi and Logan were spending a quiet evening at home. Sierra's other grandmother, Brenda was in town, so Sierra was spending the weekend with her. Logan was glad about that because he wanted to cheer Naomi up after they had a disappointing doctor's appointment earlier that day. Naomi's doctor suggested that she considered taking off work until the babies were born. The doctor explained she had three more weeks to go before she would be out of the woods to have a safe delivery. At twenty-nine weeks the babies were developed but the few additional weeks would strengthen their lungs. The doctor was worried about Naomi's blood pressure which was slightly elevated. She wanted Naomi to relax to avoid preeclampsia. Naomi was at higher risk because she was carrying twins. The doctor also forewarned them that she wasn't going to make it to the full thirty-seven weeks. Once they were settled in the den Naomi expressed her concerns.

"Honey, I don't understand what the doctor is talking about. I feel fine. I wanted to keep working for a few more weeks so I can wrap some cases up."

"Na, I think she is just being cautious. We've been lucky after that scare a few months ago. Maybe you can take the time to finish the nursery and rest up." Logan replied.

"But she is talking at least three weeks now and the eight weeks I've scheduled off after they are born. That is missing an entire quarter at work. I will never catch up." Naomi said with tears running down her face.

"Maybe you can work part-time from home until the babies are born. You know when you're at the office you have tons of interruptions. That's what I think the doctor wants to avoid."

"That may work. When I go in on Monday, I will talk it over with the partners. It will still take me a couple of days to partially close my office down."

"Ok. Let's see how that works out. But I'm taking off to help you pack the office up. I know you have a tenancy to overdo it. Remember the pains in your lower back have been better since you're not as stressed out about work."

"Work isn't the only reason I've been stressed out. It's also London. I know we need to let her handle the situation, but she is in for a rough time if Greg is going to act a fool whenever something doesn't go his way."

"I know. You don't know how badly I wanted to kick his ass when I found him over there the other day. I know he loves my sister but now I'm wondering if he is too weak to handle Lon. She has changed a lot since she met Greg, but she is still a handful."

"Yes, she is. She is also stubborn. Not telling your parents about the baby isn't right. I know your mom is going to go off the deep end, but she is also going to be mad at us for not telling her."

"That's Lon's decision. She said things are now back on track, so we just have to pray they don't have any other issues that's going to scare that fool away."

"Honey, I'm a little worn out right now. Why don't you run your errands while I take a nap before I cook dinner?"

"No cooking for you today. Take your nap and I will pick something up. We didn't take anything out, so cooking is out of the question."

"Good that will work. I have a taste for Italian." Naomi said.

"Cool. Go rest and I'll be back in a couple hours. Don't forget to have the bell by the bed in case you need Mrs. Cole to help you with anything."

"Ok. Love you honey." Naomi was glad Logan helped her to the bed. Before he could get out the door, she was fast asleep.

Chapter Ten

London woke up the next morning anxious about her last scheduled premarital counseling session with Pastor Sanders. After what they went through recently, she felt maybe they should schedule a few more sessions. They decided their sessions with Father Carson wasn't as beneficial as the ones with Pastor Sanders. Greg was so disappointed he wanted to skip the last session with Father Carson and have Pastor Sanders do that one too. London talked him out of it because his family was already on his back for letting her have too much control in their relationship. They were scheduled to go over the Do's and Don'ts of interracial dating at the session today, but they wanted to talk about the baby issue. She knew Pastor Sanders would be surprised about the pregnancy because they didn't let him know about their one time slip up.

Since she had hours before she had to meet Greg at the church, London decided to rest for a little while. She gets tired easily now. It didn't help that she was wondering what was going on with Gracey. Her surprise visit didn't sit well with London. She knew Gracey was up to something. When she told Greg about the visit after she got home last night he was surprised too. Thinking about last night, London realized after the wedding she wasn't going to be spending much time with Kayla. Their relationship had grown so far apart, but London didn't realize how far they drifted until last night. When she arrived for their date, London was surprised Kayla was sitting at the table with three of the girls they went to high school with and five men.

"Hello everyone." London said looking suspiciously at Kayla.

"Girl about time your behind showed up. We're starving." Kayla said.

"Gracey stopped by unexpectedly when I was about to leave." London explained.

"I know you're not late because of that trick?" Kayla asked.

London didn't want to cause a commotion, so she asked to see Kayla in the rest room. "What the hell is going on, Kayla?"

"Girl what are you talking about?"

"I'm talking about this was supposed to be a girls' night. What are those men doing out there?"

"I thought you may want to spice things up before you sign your life away."

"Kayla, I'm going to stay in here for five minutes after you leave. You need to go to that table and ask those guys to leave or else I'm going home."

"Why are you acting like this, London? You seemed to have forgotten how to have fun."

"I have plenty of fun with my soon to be husband. You know you are wrong for this."

"Fine. I will ask them to leave but you're embarrassing me in front of the girls."

"The girls should have understood that you don't do something stupid like this knowing I'm only a few weeks away from my wedding."

"Give me ten minutes before you come out." Kayla said rudely.

"That's all you're going to get, Kayla." London said as she remembered the evil look that Kayla threw back at her before she left the restroom.

When London went back to the table the girls were sitting alone. They didn't seem happy about the situation. They went on to order their dinner and stayed for the comedy show. London decided she wasn't going to miss not having Kayla in her life after her wedding. She also wished that Greg could have gone over to Naomi and Logan's after their session with Pastor Sanders. London convinced Greg that Logan needed more time to calm down before they met up again. When she talked to Naomi last night and found out what the doctor told her, London didn't want to put any additional pressure on Logan. Looking at the clock on her nightstand, London decided to get up and get ready for her session.

London and Greg were sitting in Pastor Sanders office waiting to get their session started. Pastor Sanders had already said the prayers. London wondered if he could tell that they were nervous. Greg seemed to be more uncomfortable than she. Pastor Sanders review notes from their previous sessions and jotted down a few notes before he got started. "Is there anything the two of you need to talk about before we get started?"

"Pastor, we were wondering if we could bypass the topic for this session and address a few other issues." London said.

"This sounds serious. Are you guys still on board with the wedding?"

"Yes, Pastor Sanders. We have come across a few issues we would like to discuss if it's not a problem." Greg answered.

"Pastor, I know we should have brought this up in our last session, but we didn't want to deal with this issue at the time. By not dealing with this issue things became out of hand." London said beating around the bush.

"I can see that this issue is affecting your communication. We must remember communication is the key to avoid misunderstandings." Pastor Sanders said.

"Pastor, I'm pregnant." London blurred out.

Pastor Sanders was taken aback since he thought they wanted to wait until they were married before they had a sexual relationship. "I see."

"I need to explain. Even though it was hard, Greg and I was keeping our no sex promise. On the night of my bridal shower Greg helped me to bring my presents home. I had a little too much to drink. It also didn't help that I was turned on by the sexy lingerie I received. I came on hot and heavy. Greg tried to shut me down, but I wouldn't listen. He brought up the fact we didn't have protection, but I told him it wasn't my fertile time. We gave into our feelings and a few weeks ago I found out I was pregnant."

"Greg, do you have anything to add?" Pastor Sanders asked.

"Yes, I was ashamed of giving in to my feelings and for the way I handled it when London told me she was pregnant."

"How did you handle hearing this news, Greg?"

"I blew up at London then asked who the father of her baby was?"

"What was your reaction, London?"

"I was deeply hurt. I never expected Greg to think that he wasn't the father."

"So, have the two of you worked through your issues?"

"Not before a brief separation and Logan going off the deep end."

"I take it he wasn't a happy camper." Pastor Sanders asked.

"No. If it wasn't for me and Naomi, he would have confronted Greg when I told him what happened. As it stands, he came over on the evening that Greg and I worked things out. It took everything in me to get him to go home without forcing Greg to leave with him."

"How do you feel about Logan's reaction, Greg?"

"I understand his feelings, but London and I have to work on these issues without interference from our families. I have problems with Gracey, but if a guy mistreated her like I did to London, I would be just as upset as Logan."

"So, do you guys feel you are in a better place now?"

"Yes, I do believe we are, but I wanted to ask if we could have one more session before the wedding. Our love is strong, but I realized the way things went down that Greg and I still have a few things to iron out."

"I agree that another session would help. I've also been working on myself. I never loved any woman the way I love London. I will do anything to ensure her happiness and peace of mind."

"Good to hear. How about you guys coming back on Tuesday evening after work? That will be my only free time before your wedding."

"We'll be here, Pastor. Thank you for all your help." London said.

"Remember to keep the lines on communication open. I also suggest you guys mend your relationship with Naomi and Logan. They are the best role models you can have at this point in your relationship." Pastor Sanders said the closing prayer then walked London and Greg to the front door.

Chapter Eleven

London sat at her desk at work the Monday following what was supposed to be her last premarital session with Pastor Sanders. She felt that she was in a better place in her relationship with Greg, but she also knew they weren't as solid as they should be. Instead of thinking about her relationship with Greg, she wanted to focus on her relationship with Naomi and Logan. After their session on Saturday, London and Greg went to have lunch before she headed over to sit with Naomi. Logan asked her to try to spend more time with Naomi because she was upset that she had to quit work soon. It hurt London when she finally arrived for her visit with Naomi to see her relaxing in the recliner looking miserable.

"Hey, Na. Why are you sitting in the semi-darkness? Do you have a headache?"

"No, just don't have anything else better to do since Logan and Sierra aren't home."

"I'm sorry to hear about your doctor's visit, but you should take this time to rest because once the twins are born, you're going to have your hands full."

"You sound like your brother." Naomi said.

"Smart man. Seriously don't let this get you down. You will still be able to work from home for a little while."

A big smile spread across Naomi's face. "Let's see if you're going to be this understanding when your time comes."

"I'm going to take it in stride. I don't care for my job as much as you care for yours."

"Enough about me. How did your session go today with Pastor Sanders?"

"We had to improvise. Instead of focusing on our final subject we dealt with the baby issue."

"That's good to hear. Was that your last session? I know it was supposed to be, but you said you were going to see if you could stretch it out."

"Our last session is scheduled for Tuesday. Let's change the subject for a minute. Girl, you're never going to believe what that heifer Kayla did to me last night. She had the audacity to set up a date for me for our girls' night out."

"Why are you shocked, London? Your world has changed and evolved while she is still stuck in the past."

"Well, I will take care of that real quick after the wedding. If I hadn't invested so much money with their wardrobe, I would kick her and her sister to the curb."

"I'm sorry this is keeping me from helping you out more with the planning." Naomi patted her stomach to show London what this meant."

"I have plenty of help. Even Colby has been nice to me."

"My sister is a lot of things but nice isn't one I would use to describe her."

"I bet you felt the same about me when I was acting a fool."

"I've always thought you were too protective and misguided when it came to Logan."

"Well, let's thank God for the new me."

The ringing phone brought London back to the present. Her assistant must not have been at her desk or she would have patched the caller through. "London Lewis."

"What is this I hear about you extending your premarital sessions?" Corrine asked.

"Hi to you too, Ma."

"I'm waiting on an answer, London."

"Nothing important, Ma. Greg and I just wanted to address a few more issues."

"I'm not liking the sound of that. What issues?" Lori asked.

"Issues that concerns me and Greg, Ma. How's daddy?" London asked to change the subject.

"Doing what he's always doing in his free time, fiddling with that silly car."

"I have to get back to work, Ma. I love you. Tell daddy I said hey."

"I'll let you run this time, but you better not be keeping anything from us. Maybe you should rethink this marriage thing if you need more counseling."

"Love you, Ma." London disconnected the call before her mom found something else to complain about.

That night London met Greg at his house. Some of the patterns came in for the designs London planned on using to redecorate the house. Greg told London she could change anything she wanted in his four-bedroom ranch style house except for the library and his man cave. London was so happy to be getting out of her apartment and moving into a real house. She knew they couldn't start on the nursery yet until they tell the family about the baby. She was starting to get excited about becoming a mom. Now that she knew Greg was on board, she was thinking about doing the nursery and picking out names. She knew it was early but there's nothing like being prepared.

"Honey, I received a call from my mom this afternoon. She already found out we extended our premarital session."

"Wow, that was quick."

"Yes, it was. She is on several church committees as well as being a friend of the church secretary."

"I just hope none of our session notes are accessible."

"No, Pastor doesn't play that way. He will make sure our sessions are kept confidential."

"Other than that, how did your day go?"

"Actually, it went by pretty quick after I talked to my mom. How about yours?"

"Just wrapping up some loose ends before our honeymoon. I can't wait."

"Speaking of the honeymoon, Greg, you haven't given me any of the details outside of we're going to France."

"That's because some of it is a surprise. You know the best parts so be happy with that."

"Whatever, as long as we go to Nice, I'm not concerned about the rest of the trip." London and Greg spent another two hours together before London went home to get ready for their last session tomorrow.

<u>Chapter Twelve</u>

London and Greg sat in Pastor Sanders' office anxious to get their last premarital session over with. They felt like a brand new couple. London had a nice relaxing night with Greg. They took the rest of the day off to go shopping for the house. They were going to go window shopping for the nursery even though they weren't going to purchase anything right now. Pastor Sanders said the prayers. Now he was ready to get started with the happy couple that sat in front of his desk.

"Wow, what a difference a few days make. I guess I don't need to ask if you guys enjoyed the remainder of your weekend."

"Pastor, we have been spending a lot of time together and we finally feel like we're on the same page. We are so in-sync nothing will tear us apart." London said.

"I agree with London, Pastor Sanders. This was a turning point in our relationship. I feel confident that any obstacle that comes our way we are ready to take it on in full speed." Greg added.

"I must say I'm impressed with the way you guys have turned things around in such a short period of time. Is there anything we need to address that may become a problem?"

"Not really. When we leave here we're going shopping for the house and window shopping for he nursery. I wish we could start shopping for the baby but since we aren't going to tell the families until we return from our honeymoon that's not a possibility." London said.

"So, you guys are going to stick to your decision not to tell your families until your return from your honeymoon?" Pastor Sanders asked.

"Yes, we are. I don't want to have to deal with the family's reaction. My mom is going to have a fit, my dad will try to stay neutral, and Greg's family will swear up and down I trapped him, especially his sister Gracey."

"That's true. My mom, uncle, and sister will go off the deep end especially if Gracey finds out that Naomi and Logan knew about the baby before the rest of the family." Greg added.

"So, if we go according to the schedule the only event we have left is the rehearsal dinner." Pastor Sanders observed.

"That's it. My parents are excited about this because this is the only event, they feel they have control over." Greg said.

"Weddings can be tricky especially when you have strong family structures on both sides."

"Our biggest battle is keeping them in check. From the engagement party to the dinner rehearsal it's been an uphill battle trying to satisfy both sides of the family." London commented.

"The couple I see sitting in front of me will be able to handle anything as long as you look out for each other and keep God with you at all times. Of course, you will have to keep the lines of commination open."

"Thank you for everything, Pastor. We better get going to take care of our shopping." London said.

"God's blessing to the both of you." Pastor Sanders said a closing prayer and watched the happy couple leave to finish up their day.

London and Greg were having a bite to eat before they started their window shopping for the nursery. They had picked out everything they would need for the interior designer to work on their house. The person they hired promised they would have the house completed by the time they returned from their honeymoon. Naomi and Logan were going to oversee this project. London was so blissfully happy. After her fight with Greg about the baby, she never thought she would be able to get past their fight, let alone come closer as a couple.

Finishing their meal, London and Greg went to the baby store. They were in awe of all the beautiful items in the store. They decided they didn't care if they had a boy or girl, they just wanted a healthy baby. Greg laughed at London when she said she prayed they didn't have twins. She knew they would be at risk of that since they both were twins. They were so deep into their shopping they didn't hear Gracey come up behind them.

"What the hell are you two doing in here?" Gracey shouted.

Turning around to face the angry woman, London and Greg were caught off guard. "Lower your voice, Gracey." Greg said.

"Answer my question, Greg."

"What does it look like were doing? We're shopping for a gift for a shower London is going to."

Gracey had the look on her face that she didn't believe one word that came out of Greg's mouth. She glanced down at London's stomach. "Why did you come with her, Greg? You hate shopping."

"People change, Gracey. I'm about to become a married man, so I have to learn to like the things my wife likes." Greg explained.

"What are you doing here, Gracey. Is there something you're keeping from the family?" London asked with a smirk on her face.

"I don't have to explain shit to you, London." Gracey replied.

"Watch your mouth, Gracey." Greg warned.

"You need to tell her that. I'm leaving now. I have to find my friend before she buys the entire store out." Gracey left London and Greg standing there with their mouths open.

Deciding that was a close call, London and Greg left the store in a hurry heading for his house.

Chapter Thirteen

It was now Friday night. London and Greg were due to go over to Naomi and Logan's house for dinner. London was so glad that Sierra was going to be home because that would keep Logan from getting on Greg's case. The dinner was Naomi's idea. She wanted to spend as much time with the families before the babies were born. Today's appointment didn't go any better than last weeks. The doctor told them to be prepared for delivery within the next week or two. Naomi was down in the dumps about this. London had mixed feelings about the babies' birth because more and more it seemed like Naomi and Logan were going to miss her wedding. They had already backed out of the rehearsal dinner. London jumped when her text came through that Greg was there to pick her up. London got into Greg's car and gave him a kiss.

"I talked to Na today. It looks like she will be delivering soon so she and Lo may not be able to make it to the wedding."

"Wow, how is she taking the news?" Greg asked.

"Not good." London noticed Greg didn't ask how Logan felt.

"We have to make sure that we take tons of pictures and video tape the wedding." Greg said.

"It's going to be hard for Lo because he will be caught between giving me away with dad and being with Na and the babies." London continued.

"I'm sure he will figure it out." Greg said grimly.

London took a moment to look at Greg. She didn't like the frown on his face. "Honey, what is your problem with, Lo?'

"I know you're not serious, London." Greg said.

"Yes, I am serious. Now answer my question." London demanded.

"Well, if you must know, I don't appreciate the way he came across to me that night at your apartment."

"Why haven't you mentioned that you have a problem with my brother, Greg?"

"Because we have been getting along well. I didn't want to rock the boat."

"I was there, Greg. Lo was a little rude but he didn't say anything that was out of line."

"Let's table this for now, London."

"No, let's not. We need to keep our lines of communication open. If something is bothering, you then we need to talk about it." London insisted.

"London, we handle things differently. Sometimes I think you are too hard on people, especially Gracey."

"Wow, why haven't we talked about this before or covered it in one of our sessions?"

"Because it's not a big problem. We had more important things to work out in our sessions.

"What do you mean by, especially Gracey? The woman has been a thorn in our side since the first day I met your family."

"Sweetheart it seems like you take pleasure in pulling her chain. For instance, that was a harsh comment you made to her at the baby store."

"Greg, we need to get some things straight right now. I'm not going to bite my tongue when it comes to your rude sister. I've learned to treat people the way they treat me. So, if you expect to have peace in the family, I suggest you have a long talk with your mom, uncle, and sister." London said heatedly.

"Calm down sweetheart. See, this is what I'm talking about. I don't want you to get yourself riled up over nothing."

"Don't say this is nothing, Greg. Let's get a clear understanding right now. We have to say what's on our mind. As far as Lo is concerned you and he need to have a man to man talk. I'm not going to apologize for him because he wasn't in the wrong. What you did was harsh and unfair."

"Ok sweetheart. Not tonight but your brother and I have to have a sit down. I want to get along with your family, so we can have peace."

"Thank you, baby." London and Greg didn't talk anymore until they arrived at Naomi and Logan's house.

Naomi was glad that the dinner went well. She knew it was tearing Logan up inside to sit down and have dinner with Greg. Logan said on many occasions since Greg's blow up that he wanted London to cancel the wedding. The tension would have been overwhelming if Sierra wasn't her openly talkative self. She made sure that everyone was a part of the conversation especially when she was telling the family about school. She was wise beyond her years and super excited about being a big sister. Her only complaint was that Naomi and Logan didn't want to know the sex of the twins, so she didn't know if she should expect brothers, sisters, or both. Now that that were all sitting in the family room after Sierra went to bed, Naomi opened the discussion with what was on everyone mind.

"Logan, Greg this has gone on long enough. You guys need to talk this out."

"Na tonight isn't the right time to get into this." London said.

"Oh yes, it is. There is enough tension in this family. It's going to get even worse when the families find out about the baby, London."

"I'm not telling them, Na." London insisted.

"That's your choice, but think about the position that you are putting Logan and I in. Your mom is going to tear into him when she finds out he kept this from her." Naomi continued.

"I'll handle it when the time comes, Na."

"No, London that's not good enough. Both you and Greg need to tell the parents about the baby. By the time you come back from your honeymoon you may be showing and that's not fair."

"With all due respect, Naomi, this has to be a decision London and I should make." Greg said.

"Don't talk to my wife like that." Logan said through clinched lips.

"Lo, cut it out. I'm so sorry for the position Greg and I have put you guys in. You guys have enough to deal with taking care of Sierra and with the twins coming soon." London said with tears in her eyes.

"Now look what you have done." Greg said to Logan.

"You better watch your damn tone in my house, man." Logan replied.

"Na, we have to go now. I promised Greg and I would think about what you said. Lo thanks for having us over."

"You guys have a good night. I will call you in the morning, London." Naomi said while rolling her eyes at Logan. She walked them to the front door then headed upstairs to bed.

Chapter Fourteen

Naomi sat in her favorite recliner waiting on her mom and sister to arrive. Sierra was at school and Logan was at work, so she thought she would have a peaceful morning until her mom called and said she and Colby were going to stop by for a visit. Naomi wondered if Logan had anything to do with their surprise visit. He told Naomi he didn't want her to be alone since the babies could come any day now. She told Logan she would be fine for the few hours it would take the housekeeper to come back from the errands Naomi sent her on. She was still a little pissed at Logan for the way he acted at their dinner on Friday with London and Greg. This is the first time in their marriage that they had a disagreement where Naomi was giving him the silent treatment. Naomi thought back to their conversation that night after she went upstairs.

"Baby talk to me." Logan said.

"I think you've done enough talking already, Logan."

"I know you not blaming me for Greg's behavior."

"Of course not. I'm blaming you for your rude behavior. For London's sake you should have kept your feelings in check. We're not going to be able to entertain for a long time after the babies are born, so I just wanted a peaceful dinner."

"She needs to drop that fool." Logan continued.

"That's not your decision, honey. "We need to support her. She is terrified about having a baby before she and Greg had time to settle into marriage."

"Well, he should have kept his shit in his pants. They do need time together before having kids so she could see that he isn't the right man for her."

"Oh my God. This is all because Greg is white isn't it?" Naomi asked.

"No, it's because he's an asshole." Logan replied.

"Logan look me in my eyes and tell me the problems you're having with Greg isn't about race."

"I don't want to talk about this any longer, Na." Logan went into the bathroom and stayed there until Naomi went to sleep.

The knock at her door brought Naomi back to the present. Before she could get up her mom and sister used their key to let themselves inside. "Why didn't you guys just use your key before I had to try to get up?' Naomi asked.

"Girl, they are going to need a tow truck to get you to the hospital." Colby said with a big smile on her face.

"I'm not up for your jokes, Colby."

"Leave your sister alone, Colby. Baby is there anything we can get for you." Corrine asked her youngest daughter.

"No, Mom. I just can't wait to be able to walk up and down the stairs without feeling like I've run a marathon."

"It would make Sierra a happy camper if you can hold out a little while longer so the twins can be born on her birthday." Corrine said.

"Mom, that's nine days away. I don't think I can wait that long."

"You're right baby sister. I'll give you to the end of this week before you pop."

"That's not funny, Colby. Childbirth is a serious matter."

"Especially when you're fighting with your spouse." Colby said.

"What are you rabbling about, Colby?" Naomi asked.

"I know you and the hubby are on the outs. There is no way he would have asked me and Mom to check up on you."

"Colby hush your mouth." Corrine said.

"Mom, you know it's true." Colby stopped talking when she saw tears falling down Naomi's face. "Na, I'm sorry I didn't mean to make you cry."

"Go get her some water, Colby." Corrine ordered. When Colby left the room, she continued. "What's the matter, Na?"

"I just realized why Logan doesn't get along with Greg. It's because he's white." Naomi said while sobbing.

"Baby what are you talking about?" Corrine asked as she handed her the glass of water Colby brought into the room.

"We had dinner with London and Greg on Friday night and Logan was very rude to Greg. At first, I thought it was because London and Greg had a big fallout a while back, but after they left, we talked and he wouldn't look me in the eyes and tell me that he doesn't want London with Greg because of his race." Naomi explained.

"I don't want to upset you baby but that doesn't sound like Logan." Corrine said.

"I didn't think so neither, but he is still angry with Greg and for the life of me I don't understand why."

"Let me help you upstairs so you can rest. We will stay here until Ruthie gets back."

"Thanks, Mom. I am kind of tired." It only took Naomi about five minutes to fall asleep when she rolled onto her bed.

London was sitting on the loveseat in Greg's living room. They had been having a discussion since the disastrous dinner at Naomi and Logan's house about whether to tell their parents about the baby. At first London agreed with Greg not to tell their parents, but when she saw firsthand how much it was bothering Naomi and Logan, she was having second thoughts. They decided tonight would be it. They will decide about what to do about this situation. Greg entered the room with a tray of snacks in his hand and sat it on the table.

"London, I did as you asked. I've thought about it from all angles and I still say not telling our parents about the baby is the right thing. I'll go with you if you want to tell your parents but as far as my family is concerned, they don't need to know until we get back from our honeymoon." Greg said.

"Greg, I will respect your decision but why do you feel so strongly about not telling your family?" London asked.

"Because no good would come from it. You already know my mom, sister, and uncle will have a field day. I feel we have enough issues to deal with without adding this to the mix."

"Ok, I understand baby. We don't have to talk about this again. We will wait until we get back to tell our families."

"Thank you, sweetheart. This means so much to me."

"You're right about the issues at hand. I can't believe our families are fighting over who should pay for what. The rehearsal dinner is going to be a nightmare if we don't do something to bring our families on the same page."

"I have an idea. This coming Saturday we will have both families over here so we can plan the entire rehearsal the way we want it. We can take the rest of this week to put the plan into motion. We're not going to give them the option of deciding on what they should and shouldn't do. They want to be a part of our life and family, so we just need to let them know what part we expect them to play."

"That will work. Now to the biggest problem I see. You and Logan. I love my brother to pieces, Greg. I can't have him distancing himself from our family."

"I will try one more time, London, but he's going to have to meet me halfway. I requested a meeting with him, but he hasn't responded. I can't change the way I reacted to the baby news, but I will do whatever I can to ease your mind and your brother's."

"Ok. I will talk to Lo one-on-one to see what's going on with him. I don't want to involve Na because I know she is scared about delivering the twins. She wasn't looking too hot at the dinner and she sounded so tired when I talked to her this morning."

"Cool. I will make the time to meet with Logan whenever he's ready. Now let's watch this movie before you end up falling asleep on me again."

Chapter Fifteen

It was an exhausting week for London. She and Greg spent the week getting the details together for the rehearsal dinner. Since Logan Sr. and Lori didn't want to be left out they agreed to let them do a breakfast celebration on the morning of the wedding. Lori complained that the dinner was a way to shine and show off and it wasn't fair that Greg parents' get all the glory. So, working on the dinner and breakfast took them the remainder of the week. The parents would be the hosts, but they were going to do the agenda and food selection. They didn't want either side of the families slighted. Sitting at her desk London thought about her lunch with Logan yesterday.

"Lo, thanks for meeting me. I know you're trying to wrap up your work since today is your last day for a while."

"No problem baby sister. I needed a break anyway."

"Lo, I don't want to interfere but is everything ok between you and Na?"

"Sure, why would you ask that?"

"Because I sensed tension from Na when I talked to her. I know it may be because she can't work, but I get the feeling it's something more personal."

"I'm going to be real with you, Lon. Naomi said something to me that had me questioning myself."

"Oh, what was that?"

"She asked me if I was having problems forgiving Greg for what he's done to you because he's white?"

London was quiet for a moment before she asked, "How did you answer her, Lo?"

"I told her in frustration that she was way off base."

"But she wasn't right, Lo?"

"I've been thinking about your relationship with Greg since you first met him. Most of the time I don't care about his color because of how happy he's made you but when he went off on you, I thought the color barrier had something to do with it." Logan answered honestly.

"Lo, you know from the other relationships I've had that problems aren't black or white. What Greg did was awful, but you know I've been through worse in my other relationships with black men."

"I know. It's not just Greg, Lon. I've been all over the place because I'm scared for Naomi and the babies. We already know the babies are going to be born prematurely, but I keep having dreams that I'm going to lose all of them."

"Naomi is young, strong, and in great health. She's a fighter too. Just like his/her parents the twins are going to come out fighting."

"I hope so, Lon. I better get back to work so I can get home to be with my girls."

"Thanks for being honest with me, Lo. I will see you tomorrow at the family meeting. If Na isn't feeling well, you stay with her and I'll update you on how things are going." London said. She paid the check and gave her brother a big hug before heading back to her office.

Back to the present, London waited on Greg to pick her up to help him with the last minute details for the meeting before they met with the parents. They decided to only have the parents there so things can run a little more smoothly. Greg mentioned that Gracey asked about how the baby shower went with a smirk on her face. He told London he had a feeling that Gracey was suspicious. London didn't care because she wanted to tell both families and let them think what the hell they wanted. She received a text that Greg was there, London went down to meet him.

The parents had arrived, and they were done eating. Everyone was pleasant with each other, but London could tell they were making their best effort. She knew her mom could be a handful at times, but nothing compared to the rudest of Gloria. She fought tooth and nail everything that pertained to the wedding. Now as they sat at the dining room table, the real work was about to get started.

"Thank you, guys for joining us. We wanted to make the last two events as peaceful as possible…" Greg said.

"Hold on a minute. We only have the rehearsal dinner left." Gloria said.

"We added on a wedding breakfast that will be held on the morning of the wedding." Greg explained.

"We don't need to get involved with any last minute planning." Gloria protested.

"You don't have to, Mom. London's parents are going to host the breakfast at the church."

"That's preposterous. Why do we all have to eat breakfast together?" Gloria said.

"This is an optional event. You don't have to attend, Gloria." Lori said.

"I don't need you telling me what I can or cannot attend." Gloria responded.

"That's enough. You two are the biggest reason why we want to cancel the wedding and elope." London said frustrated. She wished Naomi or Logan were there.

"We've worked hard all this week to get everything planned. You guys can accept what we came up with or not. We're not going to beg you guys to act like grown-ups any longer." Greg said.

"Ignore what the women are talking about and continue on son." Greg Sr. said.

"Thanks, Dad. For the rehearsal dinner the start time is at five-thirty pm. We ask that everyone get there at least by five-fifteen. Mom and Dad, it may be a good idea if you guys get there by five o'clock since you guys are the hosts." Greg said.

"We expect the ceremony to last around forty-five minutes. After the ceremony has been rehearsed dinner will start at 7:00. Ms. Gloria and Mr. Greg will do the welcoming as the host. No disrespect to any of you guys, but we have set up the catering for both the dinner and breakfast." London added.

"If you guys are going to dictate every facet of the events what the hell do you need us for?" Gloria asked.

"It's because you guys don't want to work together. We can't afford to leave anything up in the air. This is supposed to be a joyous occasion, but instead we have to take time from our busy schedules to outline something that should have been worked out among yourselves." London responded.

"The packet that we have in front of each of you is a rough draft of the menu we came up with. We want each of you to look it over closely because we have to get the final menu to the caterers tomorrow." Greg said as he watched their parents check out the packet.

"Wow, you guys did a great job with the menu." Logan Sr. said.

"Thanks, Dad. Since we're going to France for our honeymoon we decided the theme will be a French cuisine for both events."

"Why is this so fancy. I thought we would just have appetizers and finger foods." Gloria asked.

"That was a thought, but Greg and I wanted to show our appreciation for all that you guys have done for us." London answered

"Mom and Dad, we will give you the option if you want others from the party to make remarks or not. Remember we want to keep it lively and have fun while enjoying each other's company." Greg added.

"Wow, GS. They are going to let us make a decision." Gloria said sarcastically. GS is the nickname she called her husband.

"Cut it out, Glo. I'm not going to let you drive the kids away. I want this wedding to go off without a hitch." Greg Sr. said.

"This was supposed to be our baby, GS."

"It is. Now let's find out the rest of the plan."

Greg was glad his dad finally spoke up. "After the dinner we will pass out gifts. To close the dinner London and I will make the closing remarks."

"Logan Sr. went over to Greg's parents and said, "Let's do our kids proud. Welcome to the family." He shook Greg Sr. hand and gave Gloria a brief hug.

Since London was giving her the look, Lori followed behind her husband and did the same. They talked for another thirty minutes then called it a night.

Chapter Sixteen

London woke up at two forty-five am in the early morning hours after meeting with the parents. She didn't know what woke her up, but she had the feeling something wasn't right. Turning on the light that was sitting on her nightstand, she tried to focus. She sat up in bed to try to clear her head. The first person she thought about for some reason was Logan. It was too late to call him, so she prayed that everything was ok. Going the bathroom and getting a glass of water, London was surprised when she heard something at her front door. She was in a habit of sleeping with her door open. Taking the time to head back to her bedroom she grabbed the bat that she kept by her bed. She relaxed when Greg called out her name.

"What the hell, Greg. You scared the shit out of me."

"I'm sorry sweetheart. I didn't want to wake you until I was here."

"Wait a minute. Why are you here this late or should I say earlier?"

"I need you to get dressed there is someplace we have to go."

"Where are we going, Greg?" London said shouting.

"Please sweetheart get dressed and I'll tell you on the way."

Instead of arguing with Greg, London decided to get dressed. When they were settled into the car she turned to Greg and said, "Where are we going, Greg?"

"Sweetheart there has been an accident. We need to get to the hospital right away."

"Who was involved in this accident, Greg?"

"Naomi, Logan, and Sierra."

"No no no no. This can't be happening." London was sobbing and praying at the same time. "What happened, Greg?"

"I don't know all the details but apparently Logan was on his way to take Naomi to the hospital when they were hit by a car that ran a red light."

"Are they okay, Greg?"

"That's all I know sweetheart. Your mom didn't want you to drive so she called me to pick you up."

"This can't be happening. Why would Lo take her to the hospital and not call EMS?"

"I don't know, sweetheart. We'll be at the hospital in less than five minutes." Greg said.

London stopped asking Greg questions he didn't have the answers to. Once he pulled up to the emergency room London jumped out of the car. After giving the family's name she was shown to the waiting room where both sets of parents and Colby were waiting. "Mom, Dad what happened?"

"We're not sure. All we know is they were hit by a car that ran a red light."

"Was Naomi in labor or something? Why were they out so late especially with Sierra?"

"We don't have any answers…" Lori stopped talking when a nurse with a doctor called out the Lewis' family name. By that time Greg had joined the families.

"I'm Logan's dad, this is his mom, sister and her fiancé. Nelson and Corrine are Naomi's parents, and this is her sister, Colby." Logan Sr. said.

"How are they doing, doctor? London asked.

"The child is doing well. She just has minor scrapes and bruises. You should be able to see her shortly. Mr. Lewis suffered a concussion and a few broken ribs. Mrs. Lewis on the other hand didn't fare so well."

"How is my baby girl doing, doctor." Nelson asked in tears.

"She suffered the worst injuries. She's in the operating room right now. They had to do an emergency C-section to try to save the babies."

"Oh my God. This can't be happening." Corrine said through sobs.

"Mrs. Lewis also has broken ribs, scrapes and bruising. She suffered a concussion but was conscious for a bit. We don't want to alarm you but there is swelling to her face."

"Was she in labor?" Colby asked.

"No, not from what I can gather. If it wasn't for the accident and a normal delivery the twins would have had a ninety-eight percent survival rate since Mrs. Lewis is so far along in her pregnancy"

"That doesn't make sense why all of them would be together. Naomi was taking it easy and didn't leave the house much just for her doctor appointments." Corrine said to no one in particular.

"I'm sure we'll have more answers soon. I will have someone to keep you all posted." The doctor and nurse left the grieving families.

"There has to be more to this story. Lo wouldn't take Naomi and Sierra out that late without a good reason." London said as she was cut off from saying anything else when Greg's excused himself to answer his phone.

"Sweetheart, I have to run. Dad said he needs to see me right away." Greg said.

"You go ahead, honey. I'll keep you posted." London said as she kissed her fiancé slightly on the lips before he left.

Greg didn't know what could be so important that his dad would call him in the middle of the night. He was worried about London and the baby. He didn't want her to have the added stress, she loved her brother so much and wouldn't take it well if he had been seriously hurt. What was he thinking to have his wife and child out so late?" Soon they would have all the answers they needed. In the mean time as he pulled up in his parents' driveway, he had to put that to the side for now. He wondered why an unfamiliar car was parked there. Walking into the well-lit house, Greg was surprised his mom was up. She usually went to bed early because she was always up at the crack of dawn.

"Hello. Is everything ok?" Greg asked.

"No, it's not. A doctor is with your sister right now." Gloria answered.

"Is she ok. What happened?"

"She should be ok. She was involved in a slight fender bender. We just wanted the doctor to have a look at her to make sure she was ok." Greg Sr. said.

"Thank God. If she's going to be okay I need to get back to the hospital. London's brother and his family were involved in a car accident. Naomi had to have an emergency C-section."

"Sorry to hear that son. I know your sister would want to see you if you can spare a couple minutes." Greg Sr. said.

"Sure, I can hang around for a little bit. While I'm waiting, do you guys have any questions about the rehearsal dinner?" Greg asked.

"No, but I bet you're getting nervous. This time next week you're going to be a married man." Greg Sr. said.

"Not really, I guess it all hasn't sunk in yet. I can't wait to take London around France. This is her dream trip. I want to make it an experience of a lifetime." Greg was cut off when the doctor came into the room.

"I gave Gracey a sedative. She will be out for the next eight to ten hours. Her wounds were superficial so there's nothing to worry about. I took blood samples to be on the safe side."

"Thanks, Dr. Rivers. Have a goodnight." Gloria said as she walked the doctor to the door.

"Well, Dad, I really need to run. I will see you guys later at church."

"You'll see me and your uncle. Your mom is going to stay here to watch over Gracey."

"Ok, Dad. I'll talk to you soon." Greg gave his dad a brief hug and his mom on his way out the door. All he could think about was going to be with London.

Chapter Seventeen

London was sitting in Logan's room waiting on him to wake up. She stayed at the hospital all night checking on her brother, sister-in-law, and niece. Her parents were able to take Sierra home a few hours ago. They had a hard time getting her to leave the hospital. Sierra wanted to stay to see her parents and be there when her siblings were born. Little did she know she had two baby brothers, but the family decided not to tell her since it was touch and go if they would survive. The first twin was born at four o'clock am while the other was born two minutes later. Logan wasn't aware that his sons were born. Naomi had to be given a slight sedative because she became upset that she couldn't see Logan, Sierra, or the twins. Her parents and Colby never left her side. Hearing Logan moan brought London out of her daydream.

"About time you woke up sleeping head." London said.

Logan looked around the room. "What happened?"

"We don't have all the details yet, but you, Naomi, and Sierra were in a car accident. You guys were hit by someone that ran a red light."

"Oh, now it's coming back to me. Na was tired of being housebound, so we headed out to the store to get her favorite ice cream."

"That much we gathered. At first we were thinking Na had went into labor and you were rushing her to the hospital."

Logan pushed the covers back to try to get out of the bed. He winched when there was a strong pain in his side. "I have to get to them. Where is Sierra and Naomi?"

"Calm down bro. Mom diand Dad took Sierra home. She had a few scrapes and bruises, but she is doing good."

"What about, Naomi?"

London thought for a minute before she answered his question. "Lo, Naomi had the babies."

"No, I was supposed to be there with her. I'm a little light headed. Can you get me a wheelchair please?" Logan asked.

"Lo, you can't see her right now. They had to sedate her again because she was upset that they wouldn't allow her to see any of you."

"Get me a wheelchair, Lon, or I'm going to yell this place down."

"Alright, you win. I see that bump on your head didn't take away your stubbornness." London left the room to get the chair. She had the nurse to tell Naomi's parents that she was bringing Logan down in a few minutes. Returning to the room and helping Logan into the wheelchair before they left London said, "Lo, I don't want you to panic but the babies are small. You have two identical sons. Also, there is swelling to Na's face."

"Why you just now telling me, Lon?"

"Lo, Naomi had to have a C-section. The babies are little. The first baby is holding his own, but the second baby is struggling."

"Does Naomi know the condition of our sons?"

"No. She was pretty banged up. The doctor has primarily kept her sedated, so she wouldn't rupture her sutures."

"Shit, this is all my fault. I knew I should have made her, and Sierra stay home." Logan said with tears in his eyes.

"Lo, cut that shit out. This isn't your fault. The only person to blame it the person that ran that red light and hit you guys."

"We were hit by another car?" Logan asked confused.

"Yes. A damn coward because they left the scene."

"Is there an investigation. Somebody needs to pay for this?"

"I'm sure there will be. Since you guys were out of it you weren't available for questioning."

"I don't remember anything, but maybe Naomi or Sierra will be able to help."

"Come on big brother. Let's get you to see your wife then your sons." London said as they headed to Naomi's room.

London finally let Greg talk her into going home. She had been at the hospital for more than twenty hours. She refused to leave until she knew that Logan and Naomi were resting. She would never forget the look on Logan's face when he saw the twins through the neonatal window. Silent tears rolled down his face. London hurt for him. She didn't know how the babies being that small would survive. The twin that was in trouble was hooked up to so many machines it was difficult for them to see his little body. The other twin looked stronger, but he was small too. She couldn't imagine that being her baby. How in the world would she be able to take care of something that small?

It was hard enough on London to see her brother's face when he was taken to Naomi's room. The right side of Naomi's face was bruised and swollen. He was told she had bandages on the same side because of the broken ribs. Her parents and sister gave him a few minutes alone with Naomi, but they refused to go too far. Nelson tried to get Corrine and Colby to go home to rest, but they wouldn't budge. Once she took Logan back to his room, she stayed with him until he fell asleep. His mom came in for a few hours while her dad stayed home with Sierra. London told her mom and dad they could drop Sierra off at her apartment in the morning, so they could go to the hospital to be with Logan. Greg, knocking on her bedroom door brought London out of her painful thoughts.

"Hey, Greg. I thought you were going home." London said softly.

"I am. I just wanted to check to see if you needed anything before I left."

"I'm good baby. I just want to go to sleep and wake up to find out this is all a bad dream. I can't believe I may lose one of my nephews. His chances are slim."

"Let's just keep praying for them."

"It hurts that Lo blames himself. I tried to tell him this is no one's fault but that coward that hit them and fled the scene. They were lucky that someone was there within minutes to call the police."

"The driver was a coward and should be charged to the fullest extent of the law." Greg agreed.

"You better believe when Na is feeling better, she's going to make sure she gets justice for her family."

"As she should. Get some rest sweetheart. I will come get you in the morning to take you to the hospital."

"That's not necessary baby. I'm going to let Mom and Dad take the morning shift while I watch Sierra. They're going to drop me off there tomorrow afternoon."

"Okay. Don't hesitate to call me if you need anything."

"I won't. You look worn out. Go rest and check with me in the morning." London walked Greg to the door then headed back to her bedroom where she planned on getting some well-deserved sleep.

Chapter Eighteen

London took the week off from work. It was Tuesday morning and all she could do was lay in bed. She couldn't believe in a few days she supposed to be getting married. As much as she loved Greg, getting married was the last thing on her mind. Logan was released from the hospital yesterday but that didn't matter because he was at the hospital like he was still a patient. Twin one was steadily making progress while twin two was still struggling. Today was the big day when Naomi and Logan were going to figure out names for their babies. Yesterday was the first day that Naomi was able to get out of bed and walk around. The hospital wanted to keep her for a few more days so they could monitor her injuries. She didn't mind because she didn't want to leave her babies.

London wondered what was going on with Greg. She hadn't seen him since he dropped her off a few days ago and when she talked to him on the phone, he seemed distant. At first, she didn't pay too much attention to it but as she thought about it more it seemed like he was pulling away from her. It didn't help London's mood that they still didn't have anyone in custody for the hit-and-run. Neither of the families were focused on that since the twins were in trouble. The accident seemed to change the dynamics of her relationship with Colby and Corrine. She knew they only tolerated her because she and Naomi were good friends now. They still found it difficult to forgive London for all the bad things she did to Naomi in the past, but this crisis was bringing them closer.

The landline ringing brought London out of her thoughts. She didn't feel like seeing anyone, but she knew she needed to get out of the bed and move around. London answered the phone with irritation in her voice, "Hello."

"Sorry to bother you, Ms. Lewis but there is a Makayla Matthews here to see you."

"Thanks, Benny. Send her up."

London grabbed her housecoat off the bottom of her bed and went to let Kayla in. Once they were seated in the living room London asked, "What are you doing here, Kayla?"

"What do you mean. The wedding is in a few days and we haven't touched based in a while."

"I told you last week that everything was set until the rehearsal dinner on Friday and the wedding breakfast on Saturday morning."

"You need to look up in the dictionary to see what being a maid of honor is. I should have been making all the arrangements. I feel more like an invited guest."

"It was best this way because I have been having problems getting the families to agree. I didn't want to add any more friction to the mix."

"Friction. That's how you see my involvement in your wedding as friction?" Kayla yelled.

"No. This has nothing to do with you, Kayla. I'm trying to keep the peace or Greg and I will end up eloping."

"Girl, you better not do any stupid shit like that. Greg is a goldmine that will give you whatever you want."

"Kayla, I'm exhausted right now with everything going on with Naomi and Logan. I call you later this evening."

"What is the Ice Princess doing to your fine brother now. He is going to wise up one day and leave her cold behind."

"I've asked you on several occasions not to talk about Na like that. I was wrong for all the things I did to her in the past and so were you for helping me."

"No, the hell I wasn't. I would have had a chance with Logan if you didn't go all jellyfish on me."

"That's not true, Kayla. Since the day he met her, Logan only had eyes for Naomi."

"Tell that to Bianca, oh I forgot she died from a broken heart."

"That's enough, Kayla. I will talk to you later." Without giving Kayla a chance to say another word London walked her to the door and went back to bed.

Greg was at his wits end. He couldn't believe the drastic changes that happened in his life over the last few days. As he sat out in the car trying to get enough nerve to keep his appointment with Pastor Sanders, Greg wondered what was going to happen. He and London were scheduled to get married this weekend but all he thought about was the news he found out yesterday. Just thinking about it made his skin crawl. Going back to the call he recived from his mom requesting that he immediatly get over to the family home didn't sit well with him. Walking through the door all Greg could hear was his family arguing. He started to turn around and leave until he heard London's name. Going to the family room, Greg looked around at his parents, uncle, sister, and brother.

"Mother, what was so urgent that I had to drop everything and come over here?"

"Learn some manners boy. Speak when you walk into the room." Grant said.

"Uncle Grant, I'm not in the mood for this. I was trying to clear my desk so I can take the next few days off."

"I thought you were going to work until Friday son?" Greg Sr. said.

"Dad, I need to be with London. She is taking what happened with the car accident very hard."

"Accident my ass." Glenn said.

"Watch your mouth, Glenn." Gloria warned.

"What's going on here?" Greg asked.

For a few seconds no one said anything . Greg noticed Gracey hadn't said a word. This was unusal for her. Maybe she still wasn't feeling well from her fender bender. "We have something imporant to discuss with you, Greg but it must stay within the family." Gloria spoke up.

"Don't tell me something then expect me not to share it with London. Our relationship is based on honesty."

"Again, I say this is a family matter and should stay within the family."Gloria insisted.

"Dad what's going on?" Greg asked.

"Your sister had a mishap. We need to stick by her so she can overcome her issues."

"Please stop talking in circles and tell me what Gracey needs help with. Gracey you know I'm in your corner." Greg said.

Gracey didn't answer. Tears rolling down her face as she looked at Greg with sad eyes."

"I'm so sick of this family making up excuses everytime she screws up." Glenn said pointing at his sister.

"Since you're the only one that's verbal about this situation, Glenn why don't you tell me what's going on."Greg said to his brother.

"Sure, our crack head sister was the loser that hit Logan and his family car." Glenn responded.

"What." That was all Greg could come up with.

"Son it seems that Gracey been having issues and unfortunately she choose the wrong outlet to solve her problems. Gracey had been drinking and drugging the few days before the accident because of a breakup with her boyfriend. Instead of calling a car she decided to drive home. She became sleepy at the wheel and ran a red light." Greg Sr. explained.

"Oh my God no. This can't be true." Greg said while shaking his head.

"It is. Instead of making her pay for her poor judgement, Mom, Dad, and Uncle Grant are trying to cover the entire thing up." Glenn added.

Greg remembered walking out of his parents house in a daze. What the hell was he supposed to do with what he just found out. He felt trapped because before he found out his sister was responsible for the accident he wanted the person to pay. London was going to go on a war path. She already didn't like or trust Gracey now to find out she was the one who hit her brother's car was going to be devastating. He didn't know if or how he was suppose to tell London. Was this going to be the one thing to tear them apart. It wasn't right what his parents were doing but he didn't want to see Gracey go to prison. She wouldn't be able to handle that. Then he thought about Naomi being an attorney. Once she was better he knew she was going to find out what happened and make sure that person pays for what they did to her family. Instead of keeping his appointment with Pastor Sanders, Greg decided he needed to think more about what do about this situation.

Chapter Nineteen

London couldn't believe it was her wedding day tomorrow. Getting through the rehearsal dinner tonight and the wedding breakfast in the morning may not be a big challenge as they thought. London and her family were amazed at the one hundred percent turnaround by Greg's family. The biggest transformation came from Gracey. It was like she was replaced in a nice person's body. This must have pleased Greg because he wasn't stressed like he was earlier in the week.

Things were looking up for Logan and his family too. Naomi was released from the hospital yesterday. She cried when she had to leave her babies. Colby was going to sit with her since the family didn't want to leave her alone. One of Colby's friends would stand in for Colby at the rehearsal dinner. London was a little uncomfortable with how things were running so smoothly. She was waiting for the other shoe to drop. Everyone that received an invitation for the rehearsal dinner committed to being there.

With only two hours left before the dinner started, London was glad to receive Greg text that he was there to pick her up. They had already packed the rehearsal dinner presents in Greg's truck the night before. It would take them twenty minutes to reach fellowship hall where they were having the dinner. When they arrived, the parents were already there. London's heart was warmed to see their parents get along. Logan didn't want to spend too much time away from Naomi and Sierra, so he was scheduled to arrive at five fifteen just in time for the five thirty rehearsal.

Twenty minutes after London and Greg arrived, the rest of the wedding party started to trickle in. Pastor Sanders was a little late arriving because of a previous appointment that lasted longer than he expected. When he arrived and saw how well the families were getting along, he was taken by surprise. Pastor Sanders pulled Greg to the side so they could talk privately.

"I was concerned about you when you canceled our appointment suddenly a few days ago and didn't reschedule."

"Sorry about that, Pastor Sanders. I was a little overwhelmed but realized I just needed some quiet time to think." Greg responded.

"There's absolutely nothing wrong with that. The body will always let you know when it's time to slow down."

"Isn't that the truth. Now that the families are getting along it will make things a lot easier for London and I."

"Yes, it will. We better get back to the others since we will be starting soon." Pastor Sanders and Greg rejoined the others.

By the time Logan arrived it was time to start the rehearsal. Pastor Sanders had the group form a circle then said the opening prayer. After the prayer the wedding party began to take their places. Greg's parents were the first to walk down the aisle. They were the first to be seated after all the wedding guests were seated. They were followed by Lori and Logan Jr. (Logan was serving two parts in the wedding, escorting his mom down the aisle and escorting London down the aisle along with his dad). Lori was escorted to the first row on the left-hand side.

Pastor Sanders took his place at the front of the room. He was joined by the groom and the best man (Greg and Glenn). Now it was time for the bridesmaids and groomsmen to walk down the aisle. Greg's best friend was walking Colby, (for the dinner Colby's stand in); his cousin walked Kayla's sister; and rounding out the third and fourth bridesmaids and groomsmen party were two high school friends of London and Greg. After everyone had taken their places it was time for the maid of honor (Makayla) to walk down the aisle alone. The ring bearer and flower girl were the next to walk down. This part wasn't part of the rehearsal because Greg's cousin's son and Sierra were not present at the rehearsal dinner. It was a good thing because it was hard to get Sierra away from Naomi's side.

The last and the most important part of the ceremony was when the bride walks down the aisle. When London stood at the entryway of the door with her dad on the right side and Logan on the left, tears formed in Greg's eyes. Greg forgot about the guilty secret he was keeping from his soon to be wife. All he could see was the love in London's eyes and there was no way he was going to be responsible for her losing that spark.

As the wedding march began to play the trio slowly walked down the aisle. When they arrived at the front of the room next to Greg, Logan turned to London and gave her a slight kiss on the cheek. Then it was their dad's turn to do the same. Logan Sr. then placed London to the left side of Greg where then they faced Pastor Sanders. Pastor Sanders began his words of welcome.

"Thank you everyone for joining us here on this very special day for London and Greg. This couple has overcome many obstacles to be here today. The strength of their love has proven they will take any challenge that comes their way together with the faith of our Lord. Today's ceremony will include readings from the bride and groom's moms; exchanging of vows written by bride and groom; traditional vows; the placing of the rings on each other's fingers; and the unity ceremony where a three stranded cord will be placed around the bride and groom (the third strand represents God). Finally, the best part of the ceremony The Kiss and the introduction of the newly married couple."

The entire party laughed when London and Greg took this opportunity to practice their kiss. After the ceremony was completed, the wedding party talked among themselves for a few minutes then headed to the other side of the room where the dinner tables were set up and the catered food was arranged buffet style (even though servers were going to serve their meal). London and Greg sat at the head of the table. London parents', Logan, Makayla, and the bridesmaids sat on London's side of the table while Greg's parents, Glenn, and the groomsmen sat on Greg's side. Pastor Sanders rounded things out by sitting at the other end of the table facing everyone.

The table was set French style. The silverware was set in the order in which they were to be used. The forks were to the left of the plate, the knives were placed to the right side of the plate, and the spoons to the right side of the knives. Dessert spoons were set above the plate. Napkins were placed on each of the plates. The first course was light portions of liquors (champagne) with nuts, olives, and small crackers (this was designed to stimulate the senses and the appetite). No one seemed to noticed that London only drank water instead of the champagne.

Moving on to the second course which consisted of heavier appetizers were soup, tender beef carpaccio, and cheese flans. They had a choice of French onion or cream of asparagus soups. The third course was the main course. The meat dishes were beef bourguignon and chicken in wine sauce. As side dishes cauliflower au gratin, cheesy mashed potatoes, and Brussel sprouts. There were also a variety of salads. The group laughed and talked for nearly two hours until it was time to present the gifts.

London had Greg to bring the gifts into the room. They had gifts for the parents, wedding party and even Pastor Sanders. London stood at the head of the table to make the announcements while Greg stood off to the side to present the gifts. "Mom, Dad, Mr. Greg, and Ms. Gloria, Greg and I appreciate all that you have done for us especially your willingness to put your differences aside to make this an unforgettable night. Please take this gift as a token of our love and appreciation. Greg went around the table to hand his and London parents their enveloped gifts. Next London present Makayla and each of her bridesmaids a gift box that contained diamond studs' earrings and necklace set that she wanted each of them to wear for the wedding.

Greg followed suit by giving Glenn and the groomsmen personalized cufflinks. The last two gifts were important to London, so she asked Greg to bring the gifts to the front of the room. "Pastor Sanders we can't thank you enough for all you have done for us. This plaque is a thank you for the pre-martial sessions and being the best person to officiate our special day." London and Greg went to the other end of the table to present the plaque to Pastor Sanders.

"I can't believe I'm at a lost for words. Thank both of you for this very special gift. May God always be with you." Pastor Sanders gave the couple a hearty hug before they went back to the head of the table. "This last gift before we close out the night is for the best brother in the world. Lo, you've had my back in good and bad times even when I nearly destroyed the best person to come into your life. This gift is from the bottom of our hearts." London went over to Logan and gave him an envelop that had an all expenses paid trip for two weeks to Jamaica. Naomi told her that was where they wanted to go the next time, they were able to take a parent only trip.

"Oh my. I don't know what to say. We've talked about going there for our next parents only trip. With our hands full with Sierra and the twins, I don't know when we'll be able to use these but we most definitely appreciate you guys thinking about us."

"Oh look, London. You've brought your brother to tears." Lori said.

"If there is nothing else let's call it a night. See all of you at the breakfast tomorrow if you can make it." London told her guests. As everyone started to filter out the room, London took Logan's hand and directed him to the farthest side of the room. "Lo, I don't expect you for the wedding breakfast or the reception. Take care of Na."

"Thanks for that, Lon. I just want to spend all the time I can with Naomi. She is having a hard time. She is the strongest woman I know, but I see her heart breaking for our babies."

"It so funny, Lo. You guys finally named the babies but you all still call them babies or the twins."

"Ok, smarty pants. Leonard and Lance." Naomi and Logan decided to shorten Leonard's name to Leo.

"I guess it's time for us to leave. I didn't mean to keep you so long. Tell Na and Sierra I said hey. See you tomorrow, Lo." London, Logan, and Greg headed for the door, so they could get home to try to get a good night's sleep.

Chapter Twenty

London and Greg were the first ones to make it to the wedding breakfast. They'd gotten there an hour early to make sure everything was going right. She still couldn't believe that this was her wedding day and that on Monday they were leaving for their honeymoon to France for a month. As badly as she wanted to go to France, she didn't think it was the right time to leave her family. She was still worried about Logan and his family. Leaving them for a month seemed so selfish. She brought it up once to Logan and he told her to go and enjoy herself. At least there was some good news. The twins were holding their own especially Lance. Lance was the twin they were worried about since it took him a while to start breathing on his own. Leo was steadily gaining weight. If he kept up the good progress it wouldn't be long before he could come home. Naomi made it clear that she was going to bring both her babies' home at the same time. Leo was nearly four lbs. while Lance had gained three ounces in the week since their birth.

Pastor Sanders was at the church. He too wanted to make sure all was in order. He asked the happy couple to join him in his office since they had a little time before the guests started to arrive. He guessed that all that they been through they didn't care about the rule of not seeing each other before the wedding. Once they were all seated in Pastor Sanders' office he opened with a prayer and got started.

"So, is there anything you guys want to go over before the festivities start?"

"I can't think of anything, Pastor. God is truly a blessing to have the families iron out their differences almost overnight. That is the best present Greg and I could have ever wished for." London said.

"I second that. We have been so stressed out thinking we may have to get married without our families. Neither of us wanted that so now we can have the peace we've prayed for."

"I'll ask again if you guys have changed your mind about Father Carson assisting in the officiation of the wedding. There is still time to incorporate this if that is what you guys wish to do?"

"No, we're good with you doing the officiating of the service, Pastor Sanders." Greg answered.

"Ok. Let us pray before we get this blessed day started." Pastor Sanders said a special prayer for the happy couple then followed them out to greet the guests when they started to arrive.

Everyone had finished enjoying their breakfast and was getting ready for the ceremony that was due to begin in a few hours. London was a little nervous when they got to the breakfast table and all of Greg's family was there including his uncle and sister. Deep in her heart she felt the rehearsal dinner wouldn't have went so well if the two of them were there. Even though they seemed more accepting of the wedding, London was waiting for the other shoe to drop. Pleasantly surprised they didn't create any trouble at the breakfast, London told Gracey that she could help her to get ready or attend to the last-minute details with Colby. London was relieved when Gracey said she would help Colby.

Now that London's hair and makeup was done all she had to do was put on her wedding dress. She was going to wait to the last minute to do that because it was a little tight from the few pounds she gained since the last fitting. She had Kayla to help her put the dress on a few days ago to make sure she wouldn't be without a dress if it didn't fit. The bridesmaids were in the room next to London getting ready while Lori, Gloria, Kayla, and Corrine were helping her. The entire room was in shock when Sierra burst into the room followed by Naomi.

"Oh my God. Na what are you doing here?" London asked.

"What a silly question. I'm here to watch you take the most important step in your life." Naomi answered.

"You look beautiful, baby." Corrine said not knowing her daughter was coming either.

"This will be a surprise for Logan too. He promised to come straight home after the wedding. I had no intentions of letting him miss this moment with full enjoyment." Naomi said.

"It's time girls. Let's help the bride into her dress." Lori said with pride in her voice.

While everyone was busy helping London get into her dress, Sierra gave them step-by-step directions. Once the dress was on, Naomi excused herself to find Logan to let him know she was there. The mothers left the room since it was time for them to be walked down the aisle. By the time they got into place, Lori knew that Logan had to meet up with Naomi because he looked like ten years had been taken off his young life. The procession began with the church full of guests from both sides of the family. It seemed as through all the one hundred and fifty guests that were invited were in attendance.

London was the last one in the room when her dad and brother entered to escort her down the aisle. Now that the door was open, she heard the wedding march song begin. Her dad stood directly in front of her and said in a jokily manner, "It's not too late to change your mind. I can always take you out the back door while your brother makes your apologies."

"That won't be necessary, Dad. I've waited a long time for this day." London answered.

"Well, if you're all set, let's get this show started." Logan said giving his twin a brief hug.

They left the room and were now standing at the entryway. The altar seemed a million miles away to London but seeing Greg standing there with the others waiting on her was all she needed to get down the aisle without falling apart. Her dad and brother handed her off to Greg and now they stood facing Pastor Sanders. The wedding went off without a hitch. After Greg kissed London, they turned to greet their guests. Everyone was shock when they turned towards the entryway, there were three uninvited guests waiting there. Pastor Sanders took care of this problem while London and Greg mingled with their guests. London and

Greg released their guests while the family and the wedding party waited in the room where they had the wedding breakfast. They were there for about fifteen minutes when an upset Pastor Sanders approached them and asked to see Greg, his dad, Logan Jr., and Logan Sr. The ladies were unsettled by this request, but Naomi was able to calm them down.

Pastor Sanders took the men to his office where four additional chairs sat in front of his desk. Two of the men that came to the entryway were sitting at the desk while the other man stood by the door as if he was guarding it. Greg was very nervous, but he got the conversation started.

"Pastor Sanders what was so important that you had to pull me away from my bride?"

Pastor Sanders didn't get a chance to answer the question before one of the guys that were sitting at the desk answered. "Mr. Gordon, I'm Lt. Edwards. These men are Sgt. Coleman and Reynolds."

All the blood drained out of Greg and his dad's faces. They knew without a doubt that this had to be about Gracey's hit-and-run. Greg Sr. played it off like he wasn't torn into a million pieces on the inside. "What is this all about, Lt. Edwards?"

"We should be talking to you, Mr. Lewis. This is about your accident."

"Please tell me you found the coward that was responsible for the hit and run."

"Yes, we did, Mr. Lewis. I know this might not be the right time for this, but we need you and your wife to come down to the station so we can update you on the case."

"This is the worst time for this, Lt. Edwards. My sister just got married. My wife and I have to get to the hospital to check in on our sons."

"This won't take long, Mr. Lewis."

"Okay. I don't want to upset my sister so can we meet you there in an hour or so?" Logan asked.

"Sure thing, Mr. Gordon. I know that you just got married so maybe your dad could come down with your sister since we recovered her car."

"What does Gracey's car have to do with this?" Greg Sr. asked.

"Her car was the one that hit Mr. Lewis' car the night of the accident."

"What the hell. I'm not understanding this. Gracey's car was the one that hit us? Logan asked.

"Yes, apparently it was reported stolen the day before the accident. A couple of teens were out joy riding. They panicked and left the scene because they were high. They turned themselves in this morning and told us where to find the car."

"This is unbelievable. I almost lost my family because of some high teenagers?" Logan stopped and thought for a minute. "I wondered why London didn't tell me that Gracey's car was stolen."

"She didn't know, Logan. I didn't want to bother her since she was so worried about you and your family." Greg said.

"That's all for now. We'll see you guys in an hour. Sorry to disrupt your wedding, Mr. Gordon."

"No worries, Lt. Edwards." The three uninvited guests left the room with the men following them to get back to the wedding party.

Chapter Twenty-One

London was all over Greg and the others when they returned to the room. They chatted for a while then told the wedding party they could leave, and they would see them at the reception in a few hours. Now it was only the family and Pastor Sanders in the room. London was itching to find out who the mystery guests were and why they interrupted the wedding. Everyone was sitting around the table waiting on the men to fill them in on what was going on. London looked like she was a queen ruling over her people since she was sitting in the big chair the church used for taking a picture with Santa, so she wouldn't mess her dress up.

"Ok enough small talk. Who were those men that interrupted the wedding?" London asked.

"Sweetheart, they were from the police department. They came in to let us know that they found the car and the individuals that was responsible for the accident." Greg said.

"Logan how did all of this come about?" Naomi asked her husband.

"I'm still in shock. We've been so worried about the twins that we didn't even stay on top of the case.?" Logan answered.

"This not making much sense. How did the police know where to find us?" Naomi said almost to herself.

"I guess because the wedding has been front and center in the news lately, they knew we all would be here." Greg answered quickly.

"So, who hit you guys, Lo." London asked her brother.

"According to the police it was two high teenagers that turned themselves in this morning." Logan answered.

"Why did they signal out Greg and Mr. Greg? Shouldn't they have wanted to talk to you and Naomi?" London persisted with the questions.

"Sweetheart, they wanted to talk to us because the car that hit your brother belonged to Gracey." Greg explained. The room was quiet for a while when Greg continued. "Gracey car was stolen the day before the accident."

"Why didn't you let me know this, Greg?" London asked.

"We had a lot going on. I didn't find out about it until the night of the accident when my parents asked me to come over."

"But you had all week to tell me this, why didn't you?" London persisted.

"Sweetheart let's table this until later. What's important is they found the culprits. My dad is going to take Gracey down to the station. Logan and Naomi have to go also."

"Logan, I don't want to deal with this right now. I'm going to go check on the twins. Can you and your dad handle this please?" Naomi asked.

"Sure baby. I won't be down there for long. Maybe your mom and sister should go to the hospital with you?"

"That's a good idea, Logan. I will go with you and your dad. Something about all of this isn't adding up." Nelson said.

"Lo, I don't want to see you or Na at the reception. Take care of your babies. It's time for us to head over to Fellowship Hall to make sure everything is ready for the reception." The families split up going their separate ways to take care of things before they ended their eventful day at the reception.

When London and Greg made it to Fellowship Hall they were amazed at how Colby and the crew had everything looking so great. Colby needed to change her profession to interior decorating because she had exquisite taste. They had about another hour before the reception started. All the wedding party hadn't arrived yet. London knew the wedding party would be there. They weren't going to miss out on all the free food and drinks. She was glad that everyone in the party seemed to get alone and they didn't create any problems. London wasn't sure if Kayla was going to act out or not. After thinking about it for a while she thought that Kayla was jealous of the way London had turned her life around while she still lived in the past.

Once everyone in the party arrived, they were ready to get the reception started. They were going to have the traditional sit-down celebration. The guest had already been seated now it was time for the DJ to announce the guests of honor. "Ladies and Gentlemen, please welcome the newlyweds Mr. and Mrs. Greg Gordon Jr. The parents were the first to be led into the hall. They were followed by the bride and groom, maid of honor, then the groomsmen and bridesmaids.

Once everyone was seated London's parents stood to give the welcome speech. Logan Sr. started off by saying, "We are so proud of London and Greg and wish them the best and hope they will always be as happy in the future as they are today." Logan then gave the mic to his wife.

"We would like to thank everyone for joining us for this festive occasion. It was not an easy road getting here, but we made the best of it. While you all are enjoying the food and drinks please pray for those who couldn't join us tonight." Lori gave the mic back to her husband and rushed back to her seat."

"Now it's time for Pastor Sanders to bless our food." Logan Sr. said passing the mic to the Pastor.

"Thank you, Logan. Dear Lord, thank you for the food we're about to partake. Bless the hands that prepared this wonderful feast. Make us ever so mindful of the needs of others. Through Christ our Lord we pray. Amen."

Following the blessing of the food the meal began. When the entrée dishes were removed, and the dessert dishes were in place the best man and maid of honor got everyone attention by tapping their spoons on their wine glasses. The best man started off. "Greg my boy, I didn't think you would ever tie the knot. Speaking for a man who has already been married and divorced, I wish you better luck than I. Just remember to always keep the lines of communication open, don't go to bed angry, and most importantly never keep secrets."

Makayla said with tears in her eyes, "London, I would first like to apologize for not giving you the support I should have during your dating days with Greg. I come to recognize I was petty and jealous that you changed your life for the better. I felt abandon, but as I stand here today, I wish you the happiness you deserve and know that you can always depend on me if you need someone to talk to. To London and Greg, may God always pave your way to happiness." Makayla gave the mic to London. She and Greg wanted to make the final speech.

"I thank you all for supporting Greg in I on the most important day in our lives. To our parents, words can express how proud we are of all of you. To my brother Logan and sister-in-law Naomi who couldn't be here tonight, we love you from the bottom of our hearts." London handed the mic to Greg.

"Thank you all for coming out tonight. As we come closer to the conclusion of this most perfect day, I would like to say LET'S GET THIS PARTY STARTED." Greg sat the mic down on the table and grabbed London's hand as he led her to the floor for their first dance.

Their dance were followed by Logan Sr./London; Greg/Lori; London's parents; Greg/Gloria; and Greg's parents. The wedding party joined in followed by the guests. They danced for an hour before London stopped it all to take the pictures. Once all the pictures were taken, they did the infamous garter removal and bouquet toss. The party ended a little earlier then expected so the families could rest up for church the next day and give support to Naomi and Logan.

Chapter Twenty-Two

London went to the hospital to visit her nephews early Monday morning. Her dad was going to take her and Greg to the airport to get their honeymoon started. She was exhausted from the festivities over the weekend. She was so glad to be leaving outside of leaving her family in their time of need. Another concern was that it seemed like overnight she gained a baby bump. When she had the nurse to call Naomi and Logan to let them know she was there when they came into the room they looked as exhausted as she felt. The twins were doing better but it still was going to be a while before they made it home. As matter of fact Naomi mentioned they may not be home before she and Greg came back from their month-long honeymoon.

This was the first time since the wedding that Naomi saw London. After thanking London for the great gift Naomi explained that only she and Logan was allowed in the nursey to touch the twins, but the family would be able to see them through the window. Giving London a hug Naomi whispered in her ear. "It's a good thing you're leaving today. I feel your baby bump."

"I know. My wedding dress was a little snugged, but when I woke up this morning and saw this it finally became real." London said patting her stomach.

"Maybe you should tell your dad you feel like you are coming down with a bug and not get too close to him." Naomi suggested.

"That's a good idea. Greg will have a fit if the cat was let out of the bag before we get back in town."

Logan came back from talking to the nurse to tell London it was time for her to meet her nephews. The trio happily headed towards the nursey.

On the other side of town Greg was with his family saying his goodbyes before he went on his honeymoon. His parents, sister, brother, and uncle all met in the family room This was the first time they were all able to talk about the ruse they came up with to protect Gracey. Everyone was on board except for their younger brother. He felt something bad was going to happened again because the family never let Gracey face the consequences of her actions. Gracey had been a mess for a long time even though she wanted to blame Greg's relationship with London for all the problems in her life. Greg directed his statement to Gracey when he started the conversation off.

"Gracey, I do hope you learned your lesson. Please lay low and not get into any more trouble while I'm away."

"Don't you dare lecture me, Greg. All of this is your fault. My stomach turns every time I have to be nice to London and her tribe."

"See what I mean, Greg. The more you guys cover for her the worse she becomes. Now you have two innocent teenagers facing charges for something they didn't do." Glenn said.

"Shut up little boy. They were handsomely rewarded for their troubles. I'm just glad London will be out of our hair for the next month."

"Gracey, you are not to talk negatively about my wife. After what you've done to her family you should be kissing the ground they walk on."

"You are insane if you think I'm going to hovel at that family feet. What happened was an accident."

"You could have killed them, Gracey. As it is their twins are still in the hospital."

"That was going to happen anyway. I overheard you and London talking about how the twins were going to be premature."

"I'm done talking to you, Gracey. Dad, we need to heed what Glenn is saying. I don't want Gracey going to prison, but she needs professional help. I hate myself more and more everyday for the secret I'm keeping from London. If this ever comes out, she will never forgive me."

"Stop your whining, Greg. That would be the best thing to happen to you in over a year and a half." Gracey said with an attitude.

"Gracey, you're my sister, and I love you, but I will never put you before London again. Now get this through your thick head. I won't have your back when you do stupid things any longer. You can count on me if you want to get professional help but until then I done." Greg said his goodbyes to his family and left to go meet with London.

After Greg left Gloria said with tears in her eyes, "Baby, Greg isn't the only one that is fed up with your immature actions. I'm done too. You will get professional help. I will give you by the end of this week to schedule you an appointment. If you choose not to then look for other living arrangements."

"Do you see how they are attacking me, Daddy? How can you guys be so mean to me?" Gracey said pouting.

Greg Sr. didn't say anything for a few minutes. He took his wife's hand and said to Gracey. "It's over, Gracey. You have no remorse for the pain you caused that family. Your uncle put everything on the line for you. He could face prison if the truth about the cover-up comes out.

"Come on, Greg. You guys need to cut her some slack. All her life you let her do what she wanted and now you want to throw in the towel." Grant said.

"Grant, smell the coffee man. One of the twins might die. Those boys would then be facing a murder charge. Are you ready to live with that?" Greg Sr. Asked his brother.

Grant thought for a minute. "What's done is done. I feel bad for that family. They are about the only ones that are likable. Gracey and I have learned a hard lesson. We didn't give London and her family a chance and for that I'm sorry. I shouldn't have played games and let Gracey think it was okay to be mean to those people."

"Grant, your guilt isn't helping the twins and their parents. We need to pray that they survive. In the meantime, Gracey, we are not going to give you choices any longer. Your mom and I will be looking for a rehab center, so you can face and deal with your problems." Greg Sr. said.

"Daddy no. Please don't lock me up. I promised I will be good. I won't leave the house, but please don't lock me up." Gracey said sobbing.

"Too bad you guys didn't think of this before those babies got hurt and those teenagers losing their freedom." Glenn said and left the room.

Chapter Twenty-Three

London woke up Tuesday morning with the worst headache. Their late arrival to France didn't sit well with her. The over eight hour flight made her restless. She was blessed not to have to deal with morning sickness. She noticed that she gets tired out faster than normal. Not knowing what Greg had planned put her at a disadvantage, but she knew they were going to be staying in the South of France during their first week there. Greg bragged that France is the country of romance. He told her about the leisurely dinners he had planned for them, the tours he arranged visiting the villages, and exploring the finest scents in the world.

London guessed that he was up and out early because he wasn't in bed with her nor did she hear him in their villa. She was surprised he had the energy to move after all their lovemaking. She didn't remember much about their first time together, so it couldn't have been as spectacular as what they did well into the early morning hours. They enjoyed making up for lost time. Greg explained that they made it just in time to experience harvest season at the vineyards. He had planned for them a trip to the French Riviera where they could splash in the waters of the Mediterranean Sea, as well as savoring local wines. She couldn't have any of the wines, but she could watch Greg enjoy them.

Even though London planned on enjoying herself she was kind of worried about Greg. He seemed happy and joyful when they were together but when she observed him when he was alone he seemed like he was troubled about something. She had noticed this even before their rehearsal dinner. When she asked him about it he said that all was well. He just wanted to get married so they could start their lives together. London didn't want to push because she had so many of her own issues going on with the accident and all.

Thinking about the accident upset London. She was starting to agree with Naomi and her dad that things weren't adding up. Why out of the blue would these teenagers turn themselves in. Before she left for her honeymoon Naomi told her that the boys wanted to apologize to her and Logan. They were scared what would happened to them not just by the law, but their parents also. Hearing that the twins were in trouble made them realize what they did was wrong.

London also realized something else. Every time she talked about the accident or the twins Greg quickly changes the subject. He said this time should just be about him, her, and their baby. She was fine with that, but she was still worried about the twins and the toll it was taking on Naomi and Logan. Sometimes she just wanted to vent. London was about to get up to get ready to get her day started when Greg came into the bedroom. She could tell that he wanted to pick up where they left off last night, so she put everything else out of her mind and made sure she made Greg's every wish come true.

Naomi and Logan were finally able to spend the entire day together. Their parents were taking turns watching over the twins while Brenda was spending time with Sierra. At first it was hard for Brenda to get Sierra to go with her because Sierra wanted to be with her parents, but since Brenda was leaving in a few days and wouldn't be back until Thanksgiving or Christmas, Sierra agreed to go with her for the next few days. The parents wanted Naomi and Logan to spend those few days together and they would keep a watch on the twins, but they weren't having that. They agreed to take one day off only. They saw the twins that morning. They would get back to their regular routine visiting hours the next day.

The first thing they did was take a long overdue nap for three hours. When they were up and dressed in their night clothes, they then had something to eat. With full bellies they decided to talk instead of watching TV. "Honey now that we have time to catch our breath, we need to talk about the case."

"What about the case, Na?" Logan asked.

"You don't see this as strange, how the events went from no news to an arrest with details that are not adding up?"

"They were scared teenagers, Na. My bet is their families are going to punish them harsher than the law."

"That just it. I know boys will be boys, but they seemed to come from a good family according to the information I gathered. Doing something like this is so out of their character."

"What kind of information, Na?"

"Well, I had my law clerk look into their backgrounds. They've both holding a three-point five GPA in school, have part time jobs, and active on the track team. Why would they throw all that away when they are vying for scholarships?"

"Maybe that night they just got in over their heads. I was a grown man when I made that mistake with Bianca."

"I guess that could be…" Naomi stopped when there was a knock on their front door. Logan went to answer it.

On the other side of the door was a young girl with tears in her eyes. She looked to be around sixteen. Naomi came to the door and stood next to Logan.

"May we help you?" Logan said.

"I hope so. I don't know what to do."

"You're not making sense. Why are you here?" Naomi asked.

"I need to talk to both of you about the accident." The young girl said.

"I'm sorry baby. I don't know who you are, but we can't talk about the accident." Naomi said.

"Please, they didn't do it. No one will believe me because Devonte is my boyfriend." The upset girl said.

"I'm sorry but like I told you we can't talk about the case." Naomi said about to close the door until the girl shouted.

"They were paid to say they did it?"

"What did you just say?" Logan asked the young girl. "Come on in and tell us what the hell you are talking about."

Naomi and Logan led the young girl into their family room. "Okay. Start talking, what is your name?" Naomi asked.

"My name is Shelby Whittaker. Devonte Scott is my boyfriend's name and one of the persons that said they hit your car that night."

"What is this about them being paid?" Logan asked.

"At first I didn't want to say anything because I was at Devonte's house when I wasn't supposed to be. His parents were approached saying that if Devonte and his brother did something for him, he would pay for their four-year education and give them fifty thousand dollars."

"How do you know all of this, Shelby?" Naomi asked.

"I snuck in to see Devonte after they were released on bail. He told me that his parents needed the money and was looking out for their future. He's fifteen and his brother is sixteen. When their parents agreed to the deal, they were told that since they were minors, they would get a slap on the wrist, but since your sons suffered injuries, they want to try both of the boys as adults." Shelby explained.

"This is crazy what kind of parents would sell their children out." Logan said.

"Their mom has Cancer and can't work any longer, so they have been having a hard time. I don't know what to do. I will be in big trouble if my parents knew I was still seeing Devonte. It's not fair. We were at the house watching movies both nights." Shelby said before she started sobbing.

"Shelby, I'm sorry for what you're going through but as I said when you first came over, you shouldn't be here." Naomi said. Thinking about the wild story this girl was telling.

"Please. Just have them reopen the case. I know you guys may hate them, but I swear they didn't do it."

"Shelby go home. We will investigate this. Logan could you walk Shelby to the door, please?" When Logan and Shelby left the room, Naomi's gut was telling her that Shelby was telling them the truth.

<u>Chapter Twenty-Four</u>

Naomi and Logan talked into the night to see what their next step should be with the new information they received. In the light of the next day, they had to act. This was a serious situation if someone was willing to go as far as putting their teens future on the line. In Naomi's line of work, she tried to understand how people could do some of the things they do. She tried not to judge the parents too harshly but if what Shelby said was true, to put the boys on the line seemed drastic. Never having to want for anything, Naomi always tried to take a step back and put herself into her client's position. She jumped when Logan touched her on the shoulder. She didn't know he had gotten out of the shower.

"Logan, you need to stop sneaking up on me like that. Are you trying to give me a heart attack?"

"Of course, not baby. What would I do without you?" Logan said jokingly.

"Marry a hoochie mama that will hang onto your every word." Naomi said smiling.

"Whatever, what were you so deep in thought about?"

"I know we talked about what Shelby told us last night, but I'm not going to rest until I find out if what she told us was true. Two potentially innocent boys' lives are on the line."

"What did your dad say when you talked to him last night?"

"He told me I should check out the story and if it's true then we need to fight like hell to make sure those boys don't get into trouble for something they didn't do."

"What are your other thoughts? You were restless last night."

"Honey, I wasn't going to get into this with you until I thought things out. I don't want you going off the deep end without taking every logical reason into consideration."

"Ok. Now you've got my full attention. What's going on in that beautiful head of yours." Logan asked his wife.

"Don't you see it as strange how Greg's family made a hundred percent turn around."

"Yes, I did, but I thought they were afraid Greg was going to go through with his threat to cut them off."

"I don't know about that because he had been making that threat for the longest. The timing was too close to the accident."

All the color drained out of Logan's face. "Hold up. I know you're not suggesting that Greg's family is responsible for the accident?"

"It all adds up honey. The family made a one hundred percent turn around; Greg was stressed out; and Gracey was wearing a ton of makeup at the wedding."

"I hope you're not thinking that Gracey hit us and left us there to die?"

"This may be what happened. I agree with my dad that we need to check Shelby's story out. I don't want it on my conscious that we could have prevented these teens from having a criminal record."

"Where should we start?" Logan asked.

"With the teens and their parents." Naomi replied.

"I hope this shit isn't true. If the Gordons are that lowdown and rotten that means my sister is married to a monster. He is much worse than that loser Lon married a few years back."

"We have to take this slow and not jump to conclusions. This could destroy London and her marriage. I don't think Greg would be able to live with himself let alone marry London if he was part of this coverup."

"You give that dude much more credit than I do. I don't like him and for the record it has nothing to do with the color of his skin."

"I know that wasn't the reason, Logan. You're a straight shooter. My hormones were taking control of me when I made that ill-advised statement."

"You're forgiven baby. So, do you think we should call or just go by the parents' house to see what's going on?"

"We need to make an appointment with them. I don't want to involve the boys right now. I'm waiting to hear back from my assistant to see if she was able to set up something for this evening. We can go see the twins and hopefully take care of this thing tonight."

"Well let's get to the hospital so we can see our boys. I'll be glad when they will let Sierra see her brothers."

"All in due time, Logan. Now let's roll." Naomi and Logan headed out to the hospital with big smiles on their faces.

London was relaxing in a tub full of bubbles. She was exhausted after yesterday's outing. She told Greg she just wanted to take it easy today and not do any sight-seeing. Yesterday their day started off in one of the most beautiful bistros she had ever visited. She had a light breakfast while Greg enjoyed a full meal of croissants, pastries, eggs benedict, fruit salad, and an assortment of meats. After breakfast they visited the outdoor markets. While there they became immersed in the scents, flavors, sights, and sounds of the region. They were able to see local merchants set up under colorful awnings. There were cheesemakers, bakers, and farmers. There were also merchants displaying soaps, fabrics, and flowers.

In the afternoon they went to Grasse to learn how perfume was made. This museum was mostly dedicated to lavender that contained old tools used to create perfume and a botanical garden. They also visited

Provence which is known for its arts of fine fragrance, fine wine, and food. Of course, they couldn't partake in the wine tasting. Before lunch, their last stop was to Parfumerie Fragonard that offered tours that demonstrated the magical process by which flowers were turned into perfume, soaps, and other scented products. London was so glad she was able to do all of this without getting sick. She remembered Naomi telling her she couldn't stand the smells of overbearing scents when she was pregnant.

London and Greg visited the art museums to round out their day before having dinner at one of the finest restaurants in the South of France. They were exhausted when they returned to the villa. Before they went to bed London told Greg about the strange call she received from Logan.

"I forgot to tell you that I had a strange call from Logan this morning."

"What was strange about the call sweetheart?"

"Well he started asking me questions but seemed afraid of how I would answer them."

"Wow, that's weird. Were the questions about me? I know he is still a little peeved with me."

"Indirectly, he mostly wondered if you had a change in your behavior. Then he played if off saying he just wanted to be sure I was doing alright."

"Sweetheart do you think your brother will ever trust me?"

"Eventually but not anytime soon. As long as I'm happy he will keep what he feels to himself"

"Well, that's one thing he doesn't have to worry about. I will spend the rest of my life making you happy."

"Awe, you're so sweet. Don't worry about Lo. He's going to have his hands full for the next six month's or so with the twins."

"Speaking of hands full, we're going to have to arrange a meeting with the families. There is no more hiding your pregnancy. "

"I know. My dad is going to be excited, but my mom is going to complain about becoming a grandmother again so soon after the twin's birth. "

"Enough about our families. Let's turn in early tonight. "

"I like the way you think, Mr. Gordon. " London and Greg stayed up most of the night loving each other again.

Back to the present, London decided to take a nap because she was still exhausted.

Chapter Twenty-Five

It was Friday afternoon. Naomi and Logan were at home taking care of a few things while their parents were with the twins. Brenda extended her stay, so she could spend more time with Sierra. The duo was going through some bills when they decided to take a break to talk about the disappointing news that the boys' parents didn't want to meet with them. Naomi knew it was a longshot anyway because it wouldn't have been a good idea for them to be in contact with each other.

"Honey, I think it's time we went to the police station to tell them about the story Shelby told us." Naomi said.

"Do you think that is a good idea. I know we need to pursue it, but I don't know what route we should take."

"I'm not sure neither, but I do know we need to do something in case there is merit to the new evidence we received. Maybe we should check in with Pastor Sanders."

"That's an option. In a way I want to kind of leave it alone, Na. London's world will fall apart if some or all of Greg's family were a part of the cover up."

"Do you mind if I get my dad's advice. I don't want too much time to pass by without doing something one way or another."

"Sure, baby but let's talk to your dad together." Logan stopped what he was saying when there was a knock on their door.

When he opened the door there was a middle aged lady standing on the other side. She looked tired and weak. "Hello, how may I help you?" Logan asked.

"My name is Deidre Scott. I'm Devonte and Dennell's mom." The lady answered.

"Come in, Mrs. Scott." Logan led his guest to the dining room table where he and Naomi were working.

"Baby this is Mrs. Scott, the teens mom. Mrs. Scott this is my wife Naomi."

"Hi, Mrs. Scott. This is a surprise visit. My clerk said you didn't want to meet with us." Naomi said.

"That was my husband's decision not mine. Before we get started may I ask how your babies are doing?"

Naomi looked at Logan before she answered. "They're getting bigger and stronger every day. Thank you for asking."

"I know you received a visit from Shelby a few days ago."

"Yes, we did, Mrs. Scott. That's why we wanted to talk to you guys directly to see if there was any truth to what she told us." Logan responded.

"I know I don't have a right to ask but please have mercy on my husband's soul. I had no idea what was going on until Shelby confided to me last night. I then was able to drag the entire story out of my husband."

"Mrs. Scott, I must tell you I don't think it's a good idea for you to be here. When we requested a meeting with you and your husband we were talking about maybe meeting at the police station." Naomi said.

"I didn't know until last night you wanted to meet with us. My husband been trying to protect me. I know Shelby told you about my health issues."

"Yes, she did. I hope you are feeling better." Naomi said.

"I am, but I have my good and bad days. Daniel, that's my husband has been trying to hold the entire family together since my illness. We were doing okay before I became sick. Since then I haven't been able to work, and we've went through all of our savings."

"Mrs. Scott, I have to agree with my wife. We shouldn't talk about the case. I don't want it being said we took advantage of you." Logan said.

"If I may. I know this is putting you guys in a difficult situation, but I'm not willing to sacrifice my sons lives to save my own. My family knows that my Cancer is terminal. What my husband did was out of love but very stupid."

"What did he do, Mrs. Scott?" Naomi asked.

Tears rolled down Mrs. Scott's eyes. "He agreed to let our sons take the fall for your car accident in return for full payment of their college education and fifty thousand in cash."

"Is he willing to testify to this, Mrs. Scott?"

"He is willing to do whatever it takes to clear our sons' name. I know what he did was wrong. I just don't want my sons to lose their dad since I only have a few months to live."

"We're so sorry to hear that, Mrs. Scott. I don't know what can be done about your husband until I hear the entire story. We have been concerned about your sons since Shelby's visit. The person(s) that expected your sons to give up their lives are cowards." Naomi said angrily.

"In my husband's defense he didn't accept the offer until the third time he was approached. It seemed like every heartstring that mattered to my husband they used."

"Are you ready to tell us about how all of this took place?" Naomi asked.

"This person was an associate of my husband's. They didn't have a close friendship, but he seemed to know about our personal and financial problems." Mrs. Scott stopped to gather her thoughts. "Daniel said the first time they met he made sure where the boys' whereabouts were on September fourteenth and fifteenth. It seemed he already knew the answer to the question before he asked but anyway the boys were on punishment for the entire week because they had gotten into trouble at school."

"Ok. What happened at the second meeting, Mrs. Scott?" Naomi asked.

"He told Daniel that he had a proposition for him. He said that if the boys would say they stole the car on the fourteenth and hit you guys on the fifteenth he would pay my medical bills which total around thirty thousand dollars. Daniel told him no. The next point of contact, Daniel was told that the person would pay for the boys' education, legal expenses, and would give him fifty thousand cash for my medical expenses."

"Wow, but why would your husband agree to this. With a criminal record the boys wouldn't be able to get into a good college. I've done a little research on your sons, Mrs. Scott. They seem like good boys."

"They are good boys, Mrs. Lewis. They have never been in trouble before. He was told they could have the boys record expunged by the time it was time for them to go to college."

"Seemed like this person covered all the bases." Logan said.

"Yes, but if I had any idea what was going on, I would have told them no way. Even with all that was given it would never replace the fact that your family was hurt."

"Was there any contact after the agreement, Mrs. Scott.?" Naomi needed to hear the whole story.

"Yes, a few nights before the wedding."

"What wedding, Mrs. Scott?" Logan asked.

"It was your sister's wedding, Mr. Lewis. Daniel was contacted on that Thursday night which would have been September Nineteenth. He told Daniel the boys would be picked up and that you guys would be notified that an arrest had been made."

"Did anything else happen that night?" Naomi asked.

"Yes, Daniel tried to back out. He wasn't sure that the person would keep his promise to protect the boys. He threatened Daniel. He said that if Daniel tried to back out, he would make sure not only the boys get arrested but Daniel too."

"Do you know the name of the person that approached your husband with this outrageous proposition, Mrs. Scott?" Naomi continued her questioning.

"Yes, it was the best friend of the owner of the company that Daniel works for, Grant Gordon."

Naomi and Logan were shocked. Even though they had a feeling that the Gordon's were involved they prayed for London's sake they weren't. "Are you sure, Mrs. Scott?" Logan asked for clarification.

"Mr. Grant had always been nice to Daniel on the few occasions he came to Daniel's place of work. He even gave Daniel financial advice that turned out well for us."

"Mrs. Scott thank you for stopping by. Logan and I will see what we can do to help your husband and your sons." Naomi promised.

"Daniel had ten thousand dollars left. He tried to return it and make arrangements to repay Mr. Grant the remainder as soon as he could, but Mr. Grant told him a deal was a deal." Mrs. Scott continued.

"We'll be in touch soon, Mrs. Scott. Logan will walk you to your car. We will keep your family in our prayers." Naomi went to the family room and sat on her favorite recliner. She wondered what would happen to London and Greg's marriage once the Gordons secret was exposed.

Chapter Twenty-Six

London and Greg were lying in bed enjoying each other company. They were anxious and sad to be leaving their exotic villa. The South of France had been a wonderful experience for them to share. Now that it was Saturday this would be their last full day there since they were leaving for Nice in the morning. They talked about various things but when London brought up the case it didn't sit well with Greg.

"You know what baby. I've been thinking about the hit-and-run. I don't want to call it an accident because those boys should have stopped to get medical help for the car they hit."

"I know this is important to you sweetheart, but let's enjoy our honeymoon and deal with that when we get back home." Greg said.

"Come on, Greg. You don't see this case as being strange? We hear nothing for almost a week then on our wedding day all these details come tumbling in."

"Maybe it was poor timing but aren't you glad that they found out who was responsible for accident?"

"I'm not sure they have the right people in custody. I know on one hand it makes sense for the boys to be scared and leave the scene but in my gut, this doesn't feel right."

"Let's deal with that when we get back home sweetheart. We're blessed because the twins are getting stronger every day and Naomi and Logan are doing much better."

"Ok, you win. Now what do you have planned for us in Nice?"

"You're being too nosy. Why not let me surprise you?"

"Surprises are ok, but I would like to hear some of what we're going to be doing."

"Well, to start I thought we could visit the Promenade des Anglais. This is a frequently-photographed beachside walkway that runs along the coast. To the south there are pebbly white beaches that are dotted with blue umbrellas while to the north there is the vibrant city that is crowded with lavish hotels, lush flowers, and palm trees. There are also small parks with scenic squares and fountains, gardens, and ponds."

"This sounds so beautiful, Greg. I can't wait until we get there."

"It is beautiful sweetheart. You're going to fall in love with it."

"I can't wait to tell Naomi and Logan. I know it will be a while before they can take a trip like this. I wished they had done more traveling before they started their family."

"When they do get a chance to go it would make it so special. Now let's stop talking and do what we're supposed to be doing on our honeymoon." Greg said as he began to make passionate love to his wife.

Naomi and Logan sat at their dining room table with their parents. This was going to be hard telling them all that they learned about the accident. Logan knew his mom was going to have a fit. She was basically on the same page as he, not liking Greg. His dad was more like Naomi trying to keep an open mind because London was so happy. Naomi's dad was going to hit the roof and want everyone involved to pay. He loved both of his daughters, but Naomi held a special place in his heart. As they sat around the table, the parents had concerned looks on their faces. They knew Logan and Naomi wouldn't be at home if what they had to talk to them about wasn't important. Naomi started the conversation.

"Thank you all for coming over on short notice. A lot has happened this week that we need to update with you guys."

"This must be important baby since the two of you are not at the hospital with the twins?" Nelson said.

"It is, Dad. We came across some information regarding the accident." Before Naomi could continue Lori jumped in.

"Accident my ass. Those delinquents need to be thrown in jail."

"Ma, you need to let Naomi finish." Logan said nicely to his hyper mom.

"Dad, you know how we felt something wasn't right with the information we were given regarding the accident." Naomi watched her dad nod his head then she looked at the others. "Well, on Tuesday a young girl named Shelby came to us in tears. She said the teens weren't responsible for the accident."

"Cry me a river. Of course, she's going to say that. She probably was with them when the cowards hit you guys and left you for dead." Lori said angrily.

"Will you please let Naomi tell us what happened without interrupting?" Logan Sr. said a little irritated with his wife.

Ignoring Lori rolling her eyes at her husband, Naomi continued. "She said both boys were at home. On both nights she snuck in to watch movies with them."

"Why did she come to you guys instead of going to the police?" Nelson asked.

"There's more to the story. She said the boys were paid to say they stole the car the day before and the next day when they hit us they were scared so they left the scene." Logan added.

"That's bullshit. I hope you guys told her to get the hell out of your house and that you were going to make sure they were prosecuted to the fullest extent of the law." Lori said.

"No, we didn't. We wanted to check out the story to see if there was any truth to it. If those boys didn't do it, they shouldn't be punished." Naomi said sternly.

"Naomi, I agree with Lori. You guys shouldn't be entertaining the idea of letting these thugs get away with what they've done." Corrine said.

"We're not going to let the person responsible get away with what they've done. We are now sure that the boys were nowhere near that crime scene." Naomi said.

"That's enough, you guys need to stop spoon feeding us and tell us what's really going on." Logan Sr. said.

"Dad the truth is the Scott family were paid to say their sons were responsible for the accident. We've spoken to Mrs. Scott who told us the whole sordid story." Logan said.

"This is insane. What kind of parents would sell their sons down the river for money?" Lori asked.

"The kind of family that are in desperate need of money to pay off medical bills for a dying woman. Mrs. Scott has terminal cancer. Without her knowing, her husband went behind her back to make the deal. He received fifty thousand dollars in cash, the teens legal expenses paid, and fully paid tuition for the teens education." Naomi explained.

"I don't believe this. She just wants you guys to feel sorry for her messed up boys." Lori said.

"Ma, you have to hear the rest of the story. It will all fall into place. Mr. Scott was paid by Grant Gordon." Logan said.

The parents looked at Logan like he lost his mind. "This can't be true son." Logan Sr. said.

"I'm sorry, Dad it's true."

"So, who in the hell was driving the car?" Nelson yelled.

"We think it was Gracey, Dad." Naomi answered.

"Those bastards. I told you there was something fishy going on in that family. There was no way they would make a big change like they did." Lori said to her husband.

"I hope that crazy heifer is put behind bars." Corrine said.

"No, Mom. We haven't done anything yet with this new information."

"Why the hell not baby girl. I know you all are not planning on letting her get away with this. Those boys' future would be ruined forever if they take the fall for her." Nelson said.

"We're trying to see the best way to handle this. London is going to be destroyed, especially if Greg knew about what was going on." Logan said.

"You bet your ass he knew. I told her those people were snakes, but she wouldn't listen." Lori said.

"Listen, the best thing for us to do is to keep this to ourselves until London and Greg return from their honeymoon. The boys were released into their parent's custody. Nothing is going to happen before London and Greg's return."

"That's not acceptable. We need to make London come home now so we can let her know what kind of family she married into." Lori persisted.

"No, Ma. We need to table this and take care of this when they get home." Logan insisted. He couldn't mention that he wanted London around family when she found out because of the baby.

"We're going to have to think this through son. You're talking about holding onto this secret for three weeks." Logan Sr. said.

"I know it may not be the best solution, Dad but this will give us a chance to see if we can help out the Scott family." Logan explained.

"Why the hell should we think about helping them out. They shouldn't be given a break for their role in this farce." Lori shouted.

Naomi counted to ten before she responded. "Ms. Lori you don't have to worry about this being taken care of. I will personally make sure everyone in Greg's family pay that knew about this coverup."

"My head is hurting. Let's go Sr." Lori said.

"Ma please don't make this worse. We have to protect London at all cost." Logan pleaded to his mom.

"I promise I won't bring this up to London." Lori said softly.

"No, Ma. I need you to promise you won't bring this up to anyone, especially the Gordons." Logan insisted.

"I hate that family." Lori said in tears. As she and her husband left the house.

"Mom, Dad, I need you guys to promise not to mention this to anyone, especially Colby. She will only make things worse." Naomi said.

"It's time for us to head home too. We will keep this under wraps until you guys figure out what you're going to do." Nelson promised while his wife didn't say a word.

"Logan, could you walk my parents to their car? I'm going to head upstairs to take a nap." Naomi asked as she gave her parents a hug and left the room.

Chapter Twenty-Seven

London was so happy to wake up on Monday morning to enjoy her first full day in Nice. They arrived yesterday afternoon but decided to take it easy. London was starting to feel the fatigue of her pregnancy. Greg was a big help to her. He made sure she had everything she needed even when it was the weird combination of ice cream, pickles, and bananas. She talked to her parents yesterday after they arrived, and they seemed a little distance. It could have been just her imagination, but she had the feeling they were keeping something from her. She felt the same way when she talked to Naomi and Logan. But she understood they were still stressed about the twins. Her mind went back to her talk with Naomi.

"Na are you sure the twins are okay? When I talked to Ma and Daddy, they seemed like their minds were a million miles away."

"Of course, they seemed far away, you are on the other side of the world." Naomi said.

"Ok, I see I'm not going to get anything out of you neither. How are the twins and Sierra doing?"

"Sierra is still with Brenda, but she will be coming home later this evening. Your nephews are doing much better. I'm praying they should be home within the next few weeks."

"Really. That means they may be home before me and Greg. I can't wait to see them out of that hospital and to get the chance to hold them."

"I know. I feel the same. Speaking of babies, how is your pregnancy going?"

"I feel like I gained twenty pounds since we left. There is no way I can hide it any longer. I've decided something. I can't spring this on my parents out of the blue. I need you and Lo to do me a big favor and tell my parents. I'm sorry to put this on you, but I feel bad keeping this from them so long."

"You know your mom is going to give you an earful. So, when did you and Greg decide not to wait to tell the family?" Naomi asked.

"He doesn't like it that I want my parents to know. He's not going to tell his family until we get home. I told him that was his decision and when my parents find out they will be sure not to tell his family."

"I don't think you have to worry about that."

"Why do you say it like that, Na. Are you sure the families are getting along?"

"As far as I know they have not had any communication with each other since you guys left." Naomi said trying her best to be upbeat.

"That's cool. I better go so Greg won't think I've abandoned him. Tell my big-headed brother I say hey and I will talk to you guys within the next day or two."

London still felt slighted by the family, but she figured it was because of the stress with the twins. Now that she felt rested, she planned to take her shower once Greg returned from picking up their lunch. All she wanted to focus on now was spending her day with her new husband. She couldn't wait to see what Greg had planned for them to do the rest of the week.

Naomi and Logan decided to wait until today to tell his parents about the baby. They were so happy and relieved that London decided to let her family know about the baby. Now they would understand why Naomi and Logan were dragging their feet about the case. None of this will end good for London. She was so happy on her wedding day but that will change once everything came out about Greg's family. They wanted to have Logan parents meet them at the hospital to tell them the news, but with Lori's high sprung attitude they felt it would be better to tell them at Lori and Logan Sr.'s house. As they walked into the house

Naomi and Logan said a silent prayer. They heard the couple talking in the kitchen, so they headed that way.

"Good morning." Logan and Naomi said at the same time.

"What's so good about it. Your sister is hitched to a family of monsters." Lori complained.

"Ma, London is going to need our support. Please don't talk that way around her." Logan pleaded.

"What brings you guys by this morning? I 'm glad I decided not to go into the office." Logan Sr. said.

"We have news we need to share with you about London. She said…"

"I hope it has to do with why she keeps rushing off the phone whenever I talk to her." Lori interrupted.

"Ma, she's on her honeymoon."

"Whatever." Lori said.

"London is pregnant." Logan blurred out.

"What?" Logan Sr. and Lori said at the same time.

"She was planning to tell you guys when she returned from her honeymoon but felt guilty for not telling you before she left. She didn't want to shock you guys when she returned since she is showing a little." Naomi said.

"Showing, how far along is she?" Lori asked.

"She's nearly fourteen weeks. She and Greg were together on the night of her bridal shower." Naomi explained.

"I thought they were going to wait until they'd gotten married. Now she's going to be stuck with that crazy ass family forever." Lori said.

"Calm down, Ma. It's not the end of the world. Now you know why we can't rush to deal with the case right now. London needs to be home with us when she finds out about her new family."

"Don't call those monsters family. You all could have died. Lance is still fighting hard for his life." Lori continued.

"Speaking of the twins we need to get to the hospital. We'll keep you posted. Ms. Lori, we need to take it easy with London." Naomi said.

"Naomi, I know how to handle my daughter." Lori said sternly.

"Ma there is no need for you to be rude. We'll talk to you guys later." Logan said. As he and Naomi left for the hospital he prayed for London because their mom was going to read her the riot act.

<u>Chapter Twenty-Eight</u>

Greg sat on the bed Friday morning waiting for London to finish her shower. They were supposed to be going on a tour to the museums, but instead he may have to cancel because of the destressed call he received from his mom. So much had went down since he and London left for their honeymoon. Now come to find out his family had been holding back vital information such as putting Gracey in rehab, the guilt of the coverup was getting to Glenn, and their plan may be falling apart. Greg didn't know what it would do to his marriage if everything came out. They all could be in big legal trouble, especially his Uncle Grant. Thinking back to his mom's call sent chills down Greg's spine.

"Mother what's the urgency of you blowing my phone up. London and I were on a tour and I forgot my phone at the villa."

"You should have called me back right away. We have problems." Gloria said to her son.

"What kind of problems, Mother?"

"The biggest problem is that Gracey's problem is more than just drinking and pot. She's hooked on cocaine, so we had her committed to rehab."

"Dear God when did that start?" Greg said.

"She won't give us a specific timeframe, but we do know she was on it when she hit the Lewis'."

"She could have killed all of them and herself. What the hell is wrong with her?"

"That's not all. Your uncle said that he's been communicating with the father of those teens. The father wanted to call off the deal and give Grant back the money he had left."

"This can't be happening. What did Uncle Grant tell him?"

"That it's was too late. A deal is a deal. The problem with that, the husband did all of this behind his wife's back. She found out and told him to do something to get their sons out of the mess he caused."

Greg was quiet for a while then said, "So the shit may hit the fan?"

"Yes, dear. We can't let your sister go to prison, Greg. She won't survive in there."

"When are you going to realize it's not just Gracey that's in trouble but all of us are in some deep shit."

"I suggest you get back here right now. I don't know what's going to happen but if the wife or anyone blows Gracey's cover, we're going to have to stand behind her."

"Mother that's the problem with Gracey. None of us never forced her to be held accountable for her actions. Now we all are in legal trouble because of it."

"We can't change the past, Greg. Just get home as soon as you can."

"I'll be in touch soon, Mother." Greg ended the call.

Greg started thinking about the different outcomes from this situation. He didn't want to lose his freedom or London. When he returned home he was going to his attorney to see what his options were. He finally realized that it may be too little to late getting help for Gracey. They should have done that a long time ago when she first started to spiral out of control years ago. He nearly jumped out of his skin when London touched him on his shoulder.

"Why did you sneak up on me like that sweetheart? You nearly scared me half to death."

"Sorry. You didn't hear me calling you from the bathroom. What's on your mind, Greg? Please don't tell me nothing because you've been distracted for weeks."

"It's nothing for you to be concerned about, but I do have some bad news."

"What is it? Please don't tell me something happened to the twins." London asked with fear in her voice and on her face.

"No, sweetheart nothing like that. We need to cut our honeymoon short. There's been a family emergency."

"What kind of emergency?" London asked because she loved being away, even though she missed her family.

"My mom and dad had to commit Gracey to rehab. It seems her problems ran deeper then we all thought."

"I'm not understanding this, Greg. If they've already done this why do, we need to go back home?"

"There's some other family drama that's going on too. Mother wouldn't go into detail over the phone."

"Well to be honest with you I'm kind of homesick. I miss my family. So, when are we leaving?"

"I've checked into flights. We can leave tomorrow afternoon if that's okay with you."

"That's cool. Since we need to pack up and everything, let's skip the tour today. I can think of better things to do on our last night here." London said with a glint in her eyes.

London and Greg relaxed for the rest of the day. Since she didn't feel like shopping Greg decided he better go out to pick up a few trinkets for the family or he would never hear the end of it. London gave Greg a list of items she wanted him to get for her family. She couldn't wait to get home to spend time with her family. She knew she wouldn't see them until sometime on Sunday since they would be getting in late tomorrow night. While she was waiting on Greg to return she decided to call Logan.

"Hey, Lo. How are you guys doing?"

"We're good. Naomi is at the hospital right now and I'm killing time until it's time to pick Sierra up from school. She is super excited because today will be the first day she's going to meet her little brothers."

"I know she is excited. Guess what, I have some great news. Greg and I decided to cut our honeymoon short, we're coming home tomorrow." London didn't understand why Logan didn't respond to her news, so she continued. "Lo are you still there?"

"Why are you cutting your trip short, London?" Logan thought they had a few weeks before his sister's heart would be broken into pieces.

"I'm homesick. Plus, Greg's family is in crises. They had to put that idiot sister of his into rehab."

"I'm sorry you have to cut your trip short. I know how much you were looking forward to being there."

"I was, but I didn't realize how much I was going to miss all of you guys. Anyway, two weeks is enough time to honeymoon."

"I have to run a few errands before I pick Sierra up, so I'll see you when you get home."

"Ok. Can you let the rest of the family know? We're going to go out to enjoy our last night here and I don't want to call too late."

"Sure. See you soon, sis."

"Bye, Lo." When London ended their call, she got the feeling that Logan wasn't happy that she was coming home early.

Chapter Twenty-Nine

Logan was so glad when he and Sierra arrived at the hospital that his parents were there. He needed to tell Naomi about his conversation with London before he told the rest of the family. He knew London thought he was acting strange and unexcited when she told him the news. He was caught off guard and didn't know what to say. He had a bad habit of not dealing with the problem head on. That's what he loved about Naomi. She was all about taking care of a problem when it arose. He asked his parents to keep an eye on Sierra and the twins while he had a word with his wife.

"Hi baby. I just talked to London before I left the house. She is coming home tomorrow."

"Tomorrow, why are they cutting their trip short?"

"She said Greg had to come home for a family emergency. She also said they put Gracey in rehab."

"They should have done that before she caused all these problems." Naomi said angrily.

"I know right. We probably won't see them tomorrow because they're coming in late, but I'm sure she will be reaching out to us on Sunday."

"This isn't good at all. I thought we had a few weeks to think about what to do. We're going to have to tell your parents about their plans to return early."

"I know. London didn't want to deal with mom and her million questions, so she wanted us to tell them about her return."

"When are we going to tell London about Greg's family?" Naomi asked.

"I think it would be best to have her over to our house when she finds out. If she's at Ma and Dad's, she has to face my mom and all of the I told you so and how she should get an annulment."

"I agree. If she's at home with Greg, then that's not going to be an ideal situation neither. I think we need to have Greg there too so we can get his reaction. We will know right away by how he reacts if he knew about what his family have done."

"Okay here's the plan. We'll arrange for London and Greg to come over after church. Some how we're going to have to talk my parents into staying away and keeping Sierra. Dad will agree eventually, Ma is going to pitch a fit. She most definitely can't be there because she will make the situation worse for London."

"Same with my parents. They are going to want to be there too so they could confront Greg. Colby can't be there neither. She would act worse than your mom."

"Let's go tell them about London's return and our plans for Sunday and hope they won't knock us into next week." Logan said.

Greg's family met in the family room on Friday evening. They were running scared because they felt the walls closing in on them. Greg Sr. didn't like it that Gloria called Greg and demanded he return home. He told her that Greg and London should have been allowed to finish their honeymoon before they had to deal with any fallout from the accident fiasco. Now that the four of them were together they needed to come up with a backup plan. Gloria started off the conversation.

"What are your plans to clean this mess up, Grant? I'm not going to prison because of your loser plan."

"Loser plan. I didn't see any of you coming up with anything better." Grant responded.

"That's not true, Uncle Grant. I told you guys to let her pay for her stupid decision to drive while she was cracked out." Glenn said.

"That wasn't an option. You actually want to see your sister go to prison?" Grant asked.

"Better her then the rest of us who didn't have anything to do with what she's done." Glenn persisted.

"Cut it out, Glenn. I know we should have acted long ago when we realized your sister was out of control. We didn't so this is the situation we're stuck with." Greg Sr. said.

"Someone needs to come up with something because, I'm not getting into trouble over this and neither should Greg. He stands not only to lose his freedom, but London too. You know how much she loves her brother." Glenn continued.

"If that happens good riddance. She supposed to stand by her husband above all others." Gloria said irritated.

"Isn't that being a hypocrite, Mom? I'm sure you expect Greg to put his family first over London and hers." Glenn said, not willing to back down from the situation.

"That's enough young man. I've had enough of your whining. You need to suck it up and do what is best for this family." Gloria insisted.

"This is as far as we can go until Greg returns. Let's sleep on it and pray that this won't come back to bite us." Greg Sr. said.

"As I see it we're not the ones who did anything. This is all on Grant." Gloria said then headed upstairs to her bedroom.

Chapter Thirty

Logan and Naomi were glad to see London and Greg. They looked great. London was only showing a little, but she looked radiant. Naomi was a little jealous when London told her she hadn't had any morning sickness, but she was happy that London's pregnancy was going so well. They decided to eat dinner and dessert before they got into the real reason, they wanted the couple to stop by. Over dinner they both were so happy telling them about the trip. After they were seated comfortably in the family room, London decided to ask her brother and sister-in-law what was going on.

"No more putting this off. I know something is going on with the family. Ma was more out there than usual. I hope you're not keeping something about the twin's health from us."

"Lon the twins are holding their own, but you're right we do have something about the family to discuss." Logan said. He and Naomi were sitting directly across from London and Greg. Logan noticed Naomi keeping a close eye on Greg.

"Good. We're listening." London responded.

"Lon while you guys were away we had a visit from a young girl named Shelby. She told us that the teens weren't responsible for the accident." Logan continued.

"Right and the dog ate my homework." London said sarcastically.

"That's what we thought at first, London. She was very upset and begged us to do something about the situation." Naomi added.

"Na, she was probably with them. They need to pay for what they did to you all. The twins probably would have baked a little longer if you weren't forced to have that C-section."

Greg spoke up for the first time. "Guys it's getting late. Maybe we should talk about this another time. London needs to rest. We had a rough flight in yesterday."

"No, Greg we need to talk about this right now." Logan said sternly. Now he was sure that Greg was in with his family.

Naomi spoke up since she saw that Logan was in the attack mode. "London at first we didn't take what Shelby told us seriously but as we thought about how everything fell into place at the last minute something seemed to be off. We didn't want it on our conscience that these boys were being railroaded into something they didn't do."

"What did they tell you guys happened?" London asked.

"She said that she and both boys who are brothers were at their house watching movies on both Friday and Saturday nights." Logan answered.

"She went on to say that she found out that the teens were being paid to say they caused the accident. The younger brother who is fifteen is her boyfriend, so she was emotional about the situation. The older brother is sixteen." Naomi added.

"That is crazy. Where are the parents in this situation? Why would the boys do something so stupid?" London asked.

"It wasn't the boys' idea. Shelby said it was their parents. As we found out later it was just the dad that made the deal without his wife knowing about it." Logan answered.

"Why would he do this to his own sons?" London continued to question Logan and Naomi.

"The family has been having financial difficulties. The mom is dying from terminal cancer. The dad was trying to dig them out of a financial hole, which I'm sure you are aware of, Greg." Logan said angrily.

"Hold up, Lo. Why are you so angry with Greg? He didn't have anything to do with what's going on." London said in defense of her husband.

"Why don't we just ask him. Greg did you know that your family paid to have these boys take the blame for something they didn't do?" Logan asked Greg.

Greg's body language and facial expression was all the trio needed to know that he knew about this situation. Tears instantly came to London's eyes. "Greg is this true? Was it your family that arranged for those teens to take the blame for something they didn't do?"

"London give me a chance to explain." Greg said.

"Explain what. That you married me knowing that your crazy ass family was responsible for almost killing members of my family?"

"I had no part in the deal with that family. Uncle Grant put all of this into motion."

"Who was driving that car that night, Greg?"

"It was Gracey?"

"Why am I not surprised." London said.

"Sweetheart let's go home to talk about this."

"Oh my God. It's all falling into place now. Why your family did that one hundred percent turnaround, you not wanting to talk about the accident, and Gracey's committed to rehab."

"We need to go home to talk about this, sweetheart." Greg said again.

"Home, you can't be serious. How in the hell could you marry me knowing your family was behind the accident? Just leave me the hell alone, Greg." London shouted.

"Sweetheart please don't let this tear us apart." Greg begged.

"Go, Greg. I can't look at you right now."

"We can work through this sweetheart." Greg insisted.

"You heard her get out." Logan said sternly.

Seeing that he didn't have a choice Greg stood. "I love you sweetheart. Always remember the three of us are a family."

When Logan escorted Greg to the door London broke down in tears. "Why am I so stupid. I knew something was going on with Greg, but I just turned a blind eye because I love him so much."

"Don't blame yourself, London. It isn't your fault that Greg kept secrets from you." Naomi said.

"He knew how much I was worried about you guys. I told him more than once I hope those boys are tried as adults and receive the maximum sentence. He had he nerve to agree with me. How could he agree that it was okay for those boys to lose their freedom just to protect his crazy ass sister?"

By this time Logan had walked into the room. "Lon don't cry. You know our family has your back. I know now isn't the time but whatever you decide about your marriage we will be there for you every step of the way."

"That is why Mom said we can raise the baby without the Gordons." London said.

"She shouldn't have said that to you. If you decide you want to go back to Greg or raise the baby alone, we have to support whatever you wish to do." Logan said.

"I guess I won't be going home tonight. Is it okay to say here?" London asked.

"Of course. The room you always use when you stay over is waiting for you." Naomi answered.

"Thanks. I love you guys." London said.

Epilogue

One month later

London sat in Naomi's and Logan's family room with their families. She couldn't believe that the twins were finally home and that she was now four and a half months pregnant. She was half way through her pregnancy and couldn't wait until her baby was born. She found out at her last appointment that she was having a girl. This excited her because she didn't think she could raise a boy alone. After a few weeks of heartbreak, she decided that she couldn't stay married to Greg. During those weeks, she thought that at some point she would be able to forgive him for their baby's sake, but the hurt went too deep to take him back. Maybe if he had told her about the situation as soon as he found out or before they'd gotten married, she could have forgiven him.

She also wasn't happy the way things turned out about the accident. Of course, the boys were released with no charges going on their record, but Gracey was able to slide by because she was in rehab and was only sentenced to two years' probation. The Scott's didn't get into any trouble for accepting Grant's bribe. Unfortunately, Deidre Scott passed away a few weeks after finding out her sons weren't going to be prosecuted. Grant was also only sentenced to probation. This was a fair exchange to Naomi and Logan because it means the Gordon family for the most part would be out of London's life.

London and Greg had their marriage annulled. They came to an agreement where Greg could be a part of his daughter's life even though he wouldn't have custody, only visitation. Naomi made this deal for London, so she would be able to rest assure later down the line Greg wouldn't try to sue London for custody. London missed Greg terribly. She often sat around thinking of how happy she and Greg were on their honeymoon. There were so many times during her weakness she started to call him but changed her mind. She knew after what his family had done to hers they would never have a happy future together.

Now as the family sat around happily enjoying the twins being home life looked a little better. The twins were only released a few days ago. Naomi and Logan tried to convince the family to wait a week or so before they visited the twins, but they weren't having it. London was still living at Naomi and Logan's until her three bedroom condo was ready. She expected to move in within the next couple of weeks. This would give her time to be around the twins and pick up on some mothering tips. Lori tried her best to get London to move back home, but London refused because she knew she wouldn't have a moment of peace if she did.

London was happy that Greg gave her a generous settlement. His family wasn't happy at all, but London didn't care. Greg asked London if they could one day be friends, she told him that she didn't know what the future had in store for them but now it hurt too bad to communicate with him. She promised Greg they would find the best way to effectively co-parent their daughter.

London learned a valuable lesson with all the drama she'd gone through over the last few years. She will never again take for granted the importance of treating people with love and respect. Looking back at how her relationship started with Naomi she was ashamed at how wrong she was to be so hateful. She had to smile at herself because she was paid back in spades by the way Gloria and Gracey treated her. Now the best of friends with Naomi she was like the sister she never had. She also knew she was maturing because she wasn't jealous of the relationship Naomi and Logan had. The old saying is true **"What Goes Around Comes Around."**

Unbreakable Deux
Discussion Questions

Listed below are discussion questions your book club may be interested in discussing:

1) Do you think London and Greg was doing the right thing by threatening to cut their families out of their lives if they refused to get along?

2) Do you think London and Greg was a good match?

3) What do you think about Greg's family dynamics?

4) What do you think about the premarital sessions London and Greg had with Pastor Sanders and Father Carson?

5) Do you think Greg's reaction to London's pregnancy was appropriate?

6) How do you feel about London and Greg's decision not to tell their family about the baby before they went on their honeymoon?

7) Do you feel Greg was wrong for not telling London about his family involvement in the car accident?

8) Do you think Naomi was right about Logan not liking Greg because he was white?

9) Which character(s) do you think should be punished for their involvement in the car accident?

10) Who was your favorite character in this book? Why?

11) What do you think about the relationships between the twins Logan/London and Greg/Gracey?

12) Do you think it was the right decision for London and Greg to annul their marriage?

13) If the author decides to write a third book in this series, which character do you think it should be based on? Why?

14) If you have read more than one of this author's books which one did you like the best? Why was this book the best?

Dear Reader,

I hope you enjoyed reading ***Unbreakable Deux.*** This book was written as a follow up on the lives of the Nichols/Lewis' families . Diana likes to keep her readers entertained by writing something that is satisfying and inspirational. Thank you for taking the time out to read this book.

It would be greatly appreciated if you would consider writing a review of this title on Amazon, Barnes & Noble, and/or my website dianacarterwriter.com in the Comments section under Contact Us (located under the More tab). When you visit my website, you will be informed about upcoming events, publishing services offered, and more.

God's blessings,

Diana Carter

You can find me on the web:

Website: www.dianacarterwriter.com
Amazon Author Page: www.amazon.com/author/diana.carter
Goodreads: www.Goodreads.com/dianacarter

Author's Information

Diana Carter started her writing career after taking a personality test many years ago and disagreeing with the results. After talking to the administrator of that test, Diana was encouraged to submit the book she had written for publication. Born was her first book ***Broken Promises: Shattered Dreams*** which was published on April 10, 2014 by Outskirts Press. Look for the first three titles in the ***Broken Promises*** series and the first title in the ***Dark Revenge*** to be rewritten and published later by Let's Do This Publishing, LLC, founded by Diana in July 2017. See the list of other titles written by Diana in the front of this book.

Diana has a passion for writing fiction stories that will not only entertain her readers but also have a lasting impact. She loves to write and looks forward to continuing for many years to come. When she takes a break from writing, she likes to spend time with her children, grandchildren, bowl, read, and tutoring disadvantaged adults.

You can find additional information on Diana's website at www.dianacarterwriter.com, or by checking out her Amazon page at: amazon.com/author/diana.carter or if you like to personally reach her do so via email at diana.carter44@gmail.com.